THE KEY TO MURDER

A FRENCH QUARTER MYSTERY
BOOK 1

JEN PITTS

CONTENTS

For Dave, Jack, and Night
You hold the key to my heart

AUTHOR'S NOTE

While many of the places and events in this book are real, many are not. I hope you will enjoy visiting the real places such as The Presbytère and Napoleon House as well as the fictional ones I created. Hurricane Katrina unfortunately was a real storm, but Hurricane Geoffrey, at the time of publication, was not an actual storm.

CAST OF CHARACTERS

Samantha Richardson - the newest resident of Thibodeaux Mansion

Elizabeth "Libby" Tyler - owner of Thibodeaux Mansion and Artistic Coffee & Creations

William Tyler - Libby's husband

Sissy Covington - resident of Thibodeaux Mansion and nurse

Neal Bennett - resident of Thibodeaux Mansion and co-owner of New Orleans Past & Present Tours

Francesca "Frankie" Fortuna - owner of Frankie's Groceries

Frank Fortuna - grandson of Frankie and delivery person for Frankie's Groceries

Matt Parnell - resident of Thibodeaux Mansion and co-owner of New Orleans Past & Present Tours

Ruby Virtue - resident of Thibodeaux Mansion and tarot card reader/spiritualist

Connor Tyler - resident of Thibodeaux Mansion, son of Libby and William, and restaurant manager

Andrew Ballard - resident of Thibodeaux Mansion and owner of Lagniappe Books

Joey Martin - friend of Neal's and grad student

1

———

"Here's your key, Sammy. You're officially one of us, darlin'!"

My life in New Orleans started off with those words. Short, sweet, and full of unending positivity, Elizabeth Tyler, Libby for short, handed me the key to my new home in Thibodeaux Mansion, a former single-family home. This French Quarter building held seven apartments of which number four was now mine.

"She means you're one of us in the building. It will take decades before you're considered a resident of the city," her husband said, which fit his demeanor and physical presence. William was tall to Libby's shortness, gruff to her sweetness, and practical to his wife's often impractical nature.

"William! Don't scare her off already." Libby swatted her husband's arm as she pulled him toward the door. "Now remember, we're in number two. I think I've put everything in here that you'll need, but ask me for anything else. We'll see you later."

Exhausted from traveling, and a bit overwhelmed that I

was here, I flopped on the love seat. "Thirty is the new twenty," my best friend, Madeline Collins, insisted when I complained on my birthday that my life wasn't going anywhere. With no real career, no boyfriend, and no strong ties to the area, I needed to make a drastic change if I wanted a different life. After the third martini we made a plan for me to move from San Francisco to New Orleans.

"New Orleans?" Madeline said after finishing her martini. "I thought you'd pick Los Angeles, somewhere closer to me."

"You know why," I said while waving off another drink from the bartender.

"Of course, your parents, but they weren't from there."

"No, they grew up in Baton Rouge, but New Orleans is more my kind of place."

Madeline didn't argue with me as she knew of my obsession with all things New Orleans. From the history, music, food, and culture, I read, listened, and devoured anything related to the city. Although my parents adopted me in Louisiana, we never visited as much as I begged them. Now that it had been over a year since their deaths, my grief and loyalty wasn't holding me back from my dreams of living in New Orleans.

And that's how I ended up in this furnished apartment in the French Quarter.

I let out a sigh of relief as I looked around my living room. It was only my second time here. I chose this place, or rather it picked me, on my weekend trip to find a new home. I flew in on a Friday and meandered the streets until I found Libby's shop, Artistic Coffee & Creations, on a Saturday. An hour of chatting and two café au laits later, I followed Libby here. I said yes even before I entered the apartment.

Thibodeaux Mansion was quintessentially French

Quarter with its wrought-iron balconies and dark green shutters decorating the bright coral home. A few steps through the old carriage entrance and I was enchanted. The slate pathway led the whole length of the main building and the former slave quarters to a lush garden. Halfway to the back of the courtyard was the door to my apartment, one of four, inside the former slave quarters. My door opened to a small living room with a faded, but comfortable love seat, and a scuffed wooden coffee table.

Books filled the shelves, while New Orleans themed artwork lined the redbrick walls. To the left of the living room was a galley kitchen, which was plenty big for me, the incompetent cook. Walking through the kitchen, I entered the cozy bedroom with a classic four-poster bed, nightstand, and dresser. The small, but quaint bathroom finished my new home. My deposit check and a warm embrace sealed the deal with Libby.

Since I didn't bring much with me, my landlords left only two shelves empty. I picked up one of my boxes and moved it over to the bookshelves which held an eclectic array of books from New Orleans-inspired authors like Anne Rice, William Faulkner, and Tennessee Williams. A book with no title on the spine was sticking out farther than the rest, but before I could push it back into place, I heard a firm knock from the courtyard. I opened my door to a large fruit basket in my face.

"Neal, get off that annoying skateboard and come say hi," yelled the fruit basket. "Oh, sorry, where are my manners?" The basket was thrust into my hands, revealing a woman who appeared to be my age, but whose authoritative tone made me think she was older. I took in her crisp navy-blue scrubs, golden hair pulled into a disciplined ponytail, and a surprising dash of bright pink lipstick. I liked her already.

"I am so sorry! I really don't mean to yell in your face, especially on your first day here. Neal doesn't know when to stop when he's on that skateboard."

"No worries. Is he your son?"

"Oh my, Neal Bennett is another renter! He's twenty-nine going on nine. Get your butt over here and meet our new friend. I'm Sissy Covington, one of your upstairs neighbors."

An empty skateboard flew by. A lanky man wearing blue cargo shorts, a bright yellow "New Orleans Past & Present Tours" T-shirt, and a mischievous grin followed it. "You must be Neal," I said as he stopped at my door.

"Smart and sexy! I like our new neighbor, Sissy," Neal replied. He brushed his long brown hair out of his eyes before he reached out to shake my hand.

I shifted the basket to my hip, so I could return his handshake. My travel outfit of jeans, a black V-neck sweater, faded pink Converse sneakers, and my strawberry-blonde hair escaping out of a haphazard bun didn't scream smart and sexy. I hoped Neal was being polite and not sarcastic. Before I could respond, Sissy scolded him.

"Please use your manners! Yes, she is cute, but remember what happened the last time you put the moves on a neighbor. Her bodybuilder fiancé almost—"

"Let's not share that tale yet," a red-faced Neal interrupted as he turned to face me. "So, what's your story? Where are you from? Do you like it here? Have a boyfriend? Do you have a name?"

Normally, I would have been surprised by his deluge of questions, but his Southern charm relaxed me right away. In all the places I've lived, I'd never had this much interaction with my neighbors, especially in the first hour.

"I'm Samantha Richardson. Just moved from San Francisco. I'm single and ready to mingle." I giggled as soon as that last sentence came out of my mouth. I was embarrassed, but thankfully my new neighbors enjoyed it.

"You'll fit right in, Sammy!" he hollered as he ran to grab his skateboard. "I have to do a tour, but meet me at The Gas Light bar. Sissy will give you directions!" With a smooth push of his skateboard, Neal maneuvered out onto the street and disappeared in a flash.

"Now, Sammy, Neal is crazy, but in a good way, I swear."

"He seems like a lot of fun," I said. "You're kind to bring this gift, but how did you know I moved in?"

"Oh, honey, Libby tells everyone everything. She didn't tell you about us?"

"No. She only mentioned that she and William had an adult son who lived in the building."

"She'll fill you in soon enough. I wish I could talk, but I have to go to the hospital," she said as she checked her watch. "I'm a nurse, and I work strange hours, but if you need anything, let me know."

"Thanks, I really appreciate it." I meant it. The reality was I was thousands of miles away from the life I knew. It was hitting me harder than I expected. "I don't know much about New Orleans, so I'll take all the help I can get."

"Getting the lay of the land is part of the fun of moving here. First, start with The Gas Light on Chartres Street. Neal's usually there around eight thirty, so that gives you a few hours to settle in," Sissy said as she walked toward the gate. "They only serve stale peanuts, so eat some of that fruit before you go. Everyone will want to buy the new neighbor a drink!"

As I put my housewarming gift on the kitchen counter, it hit me that everybody here called me Sammy. That was strange since no one ever used that nickname. Was this a Southern thing? And was Sissy really her name, or was it short for something? And did Neal give tours on his skateboard? And what else did Libby say about me?

I would find out the answers to all these questions eventually if this interaction was any indication of the level of friendliness of my new neighbors. Southern hospitality was a real thing, not just an urban legend.

While I was eager to make friends, my original plan was to curl up with the new mystery book I bought a month ago. Apparently, my neighbors assumed I would go out tonight. Were they being a bit pushy, expecting me to show up by myself at a bar?

No. It was their friendly nature, or at least that's what I would believe for now. Sissy's warning about stale peanuts and my growling stomach made it clear I needed to get food first. While the fruit basket was lovely, I wanted something more substantial before I went out for drinks. After redoing my messy bun, I grabbed my backpack and keys and forced myself outside and into my new life.

2

———

Once I stepped out onto the street, I was happy that I left my apartment. While this was only my second time here, I loved this town already, especially the French Quarter. I adored the mix of three-story brick buildings fitted with wrought-iron balconies and the brightly painted cottages that lined the streets. Something intrigued me about the houses that kept their shutters open. I enjoyed peering in and seeing a bit of the owner's life. Equally I liked the shuttered homes for the mysterious stories I imagined behind the windows.

I also loved peeking into the courtyards. Although most were hidden by houses, some were visible from side alleys or front entrances like my building. The courtyards' bits of greenery, patio furniture, bicycles, and water fountains seen through their protective gates added to their mystery. Again, more fodder for my imaginary stories about each place and the lives of the people who lived there.

I should have researched the neighborhood more before I left, but I assumed I would run into a corner grocery store at some point. Libby's coffee shop was the opposite direction, and although I loved her pastries, I knew my scale would not.

Instead of searching for stores on my phone, I used it as a camera. There were just too many great photos to take. I promised my San Francisco friends and former coworkers I would keep my Facebook and Instagram accounts up to date, so I needed to pick something to start with. I settled on a picture of the white ceramic tiles with blue letters, embedded in the sidewalk, that spelled out Royal for the street name.

I included the tips of my shoes to make it a "proof of life" photo. I knew some of my San Francisco friends still didn't believe this was a permanent move. "You'll be back" was a common phrase among my friends. They were wrong since there was nothing keeping me in San Francisco, so there really was nothing to make me come back.

I intended New Orleans to be my hometown. Unless things went wrong here, but my gut told me it wouldn't. And if it didn't work out, I would just try again somewhere else. Easier said than done.

Rather than dwelling on the negative, I focused on uploading my photo. I posted it with the caption, "Feet on the ground, head in the clouds. I made it to New Orleans!" It wasn't the smartest idea to type and walk since I collided into a woman in front of me.

"Oh, I'm sorry! I wasn't paying attention to what I was doing."

I could have used her petite stature as the reason for running into her, but she was only small in size. From her wide, warm smile to the bright pink dress, she stood out even if she was tiny.

"My dear, it's no problem. You've got a city walk going on, though," she said. "Where are you going in such a rush?"

City walk? I guess I was walking with a purpose like I did in San Francisco. I would have to learn to slow it down here. And really, I wasn't in a hurry, just hungry.

"I need to find a grocery store. Do you have any suggestions?"

"New to the neighborhood? Welcome, my friend. I will take you to the best corner store in the Quarter. But I'll tell you, I'm biased because it's mine. Come with me!"

We exchanged names as we walked a few blocks to her place. She was the owner of Frankie's Groceries. Francesca Fortuna was her given name, but her friends and family called her Frankie. I felt her love of the Quarter just from the few stories she shared as we strolled to her shop.

"My life is in this neighborhood," she said as she opened the door. "Come in and meet my grandson, Frank. He works with me. Such a sweet boy."

"How's Mr. Robert today?" he asked as she took his place behind the counter and put a no-nonsense white apron over her dress.

"Oh, as good as can be with his gout. My lasagna will make him right."

"Always does," he replied. "A delivery order came in while you were gone, so I'm heading out." He grabbed two large grocery bags while kissing his grandmother on the cheek.

"That's my boy. Say hi to our new friend, Miss Sammy, before you go. She's one of Miss Libby's new tenants."

"Welcome to the neighborhood," Frank said as he turned to look at me. He put his bags pack down on the counter and took the toothpick he was chewing on out of his mouth. "Well, hello, Miss Sammy. It's nice to have such a beautiful new addition to our community."

"I'm glad to be here," I answered as I tried to remove my

hand from his tight handshake. While he looked like Frankie's namesake with her bright green eyes, short brown hair, and engaging smile, his friendliness didn't exude the same sincerity as his grandmother's.

"Frank, you better hurry or you'll be late," Frankie said as she pointed at the door. "You'll see Miss Sammy again."

"I hope so." He winked as he put his toothpick back in his mouth and rushed out of the store. If he hadn't spoken with such a thick Southern drawl, I would have sworn I was still in San Francisco with the overly flirtatious men.

"Frank is a softie when it comes to pretty girls. He is single, though."

I smiled at Frankie's matchmaking attempt, but changed the subject, as romance was the last thing on my mind, although Frank was handsome. But food was more important, so I focused on my grocery shopping.

It was your typical convenience store, but with more of the basic necessities for carless residents of the neighborhood of which I was now one. With the diverse menu, I could eat here for days. Frankie's Italian roots showed with her offerings of ravioli and manicotti, alongside Southern classics like po-boy sandwiches and crawfish étouffée.

I shopped for a few pantry items and treats from the deli, including a classic muffuletta sandwich. I planned to try them every place I could in New Orleans. It could be a great blog, "The Girl and the Sandwich." Or was it too cheesy?

"I put our menu in your bag, so if you want to order by phone, I'll send Frank to deliver. But do come and see me when you can, city girl," Frankie said as she handed me my bags.

After promising my new friend I would visit her soon, I left the shop with my groceries and a slower-paced walk. It felt awkward, but there was something to be said for this new stride as I discovered other courtyards and windows.

I entered my building's courtyard to find a woman standing by the bistro table under the living room window of my apartment. Swathed head to toe in soft layers of lilac and silver, she turned as I walked in her direction. She tapped a ring-laden hand on the table as her deeply lined face jutted toward me.

"Why would you put them here? Do you have any idea how dangerous these are?"

She pointed at a large vase filled with my favorite flowers, stargazer lilies. The arrangement didn't appear problematic, but I saw nothing else on the table.

"I'm sorry, but I don't know what you're talking about." As I came closer the woman stepped back so abruptly, I assumed I startled her.

"I hope you're being honest. Your energy is puzzling."

I ignored her strange remark as I pulled a card from the arrangement and replied, "These flowers are from my former coworkers. I live here. How about you?"

"You're the new neighbor." She sighed. "I should have known Libby would rent the apartment without vetting your spirit. I have asked her repeatedly to let me examine the new renters first."

Vetting my spirit? Was this the New Age version of a credit check? I thought better than to say that to the agitated stranger and instead said, "I'm confused. Do you live here?"

"Yes. I am your neighbor." She pointed to the apartment next to mine, closest to the back of the courtyard. "I have lived there for many years. I expect the utmost courtesy and respect from you."

I tried to interject that I was always a good neighbor, but she didn't give me a chance.

"Young lady, I can see that you are here for an adventure, but don't make me any part of it. There is something strange about your aura, so I need you to keep your spirit and your troubles to yourself."

"Excuse me? Troubles?"

She disregarded my questions and grabbed the bouquet from my table. "First thing you must do is take these flowers inside. They are poisonous to cats, and I don't want my babies anywhere near them."

On cue, two slinky black cats strolled from the garden and sat like statues at her front door. Would she ride off on a broom next?

"I'll bring the flowers inside," I said. "What beautiful cats you have. I'm Samantha Richardson and you are?" I stuck out my hand to shake hers, intending to kill her with kindness, but instead she placed the vase in my hands. With a swish of her layers and a curt nod of her head, she sashayed to her front door.

"I don't know yet if trouble follows you or if you invite it in. Time will tell."

And with those words, my new neighbor and her cats disappeared into her apartment, leaving me dumbfounded, holding supposedly deadly flowers, and a lot of questions.

3

———

I'd lived next to strange people, but no one had made a scene like that at our first meeting. Or any other meeting. Was she the reason Libby didn't tell me about the other neighbors? Maybe this woman was just being dramatic. The Southern charm I experienced earlier didn't extend to her.

I tried to shake off our encounter by putting my groceries away and eating the muffuletta from Frankie's store. I could only eat half the sandwich which was filled with layers of rich meats and cheese topped with a salty olive salad. After finishing it with a bag of Zapp's chips and a Diet Coke, I definitely needed to write that blog.

With a full belly my energy and mood lifted. I wandered over to the bookshelf I investigated earlier. I tried to push the untitled book back in to line up with the other books, but it wouldn't budge. Taking it off the shelf, I realized it was out of shape from a key on a long chain inside.

The chain was ordinary, just brass-colored with no clasp. The key was another story. Almost three inches long, it was a darker brass with a touch of green patina throughout. On one end of the key was an oval with an upside-down heart on the outside. A filigree design filled the oval, not too ornate, but not too plain. The part of the key that fit into the lock looked like a four-step staircase. I had never seen anything like it.

The book that held the key didn't have a title or author on the red leather cover either. I turned it over to see if the key went to a lock for it. There was no lock, but it was a diary. The first entry was this:

October 1st

    I have met my true love today. After what felt like an eternity, the handsome stranger introduced himself. He's as smart and kind as I imagined, a true Southern gentleman. I can't wait to see where this relationship goes...

I MUST HAVE FOUND someone's diary or at least the story of their love life.

October 3rd

    Today was amazing as my handsome stranger is even more fun than I imagined. He is going to teach me about New Orleans through riddles like a scavenger hunt. I will write the clues down in my diary so I can share them with our future children. Perhaps I'm jumping the gun, but I don't care. I have never been this happy!

FROM THE LABORED CURSIVE HANDWRITING, and occasional specks of blue ink, I didn't get the impression that the writer was comfortable writing in script. I guessed she was trying her best to make her penmanship appear fancier than her skills allowed.

Was this a diary or a New Orleans tour guide book done as a scavenger hunt? If it was a scavenger hunt, I was all in. I loved them from childhood to adulthood. Between hunts, and the now popular escape rooms, my friends always brought me along to solve them.

And while mystery novels were my passion, my guilty pleasure were romantic comedies. My friends enjoyed teasing me, asking which I liked better: romance or murder. I would always answer that it depended on the day or the person.

This book could be a fun way to explore the city, but since it read like a diary, I thought I should check for its owner with Libby. It would have to wait until later as I needed to get ready to go out. Whether it was an invitation or a summons, I wanted to be presentable and prompt for my first night out.

4

After searching the same block three times, I thought Sissy and Neal must be hazing me. I assumed every bar in the Quarter had neon signs, but The Gas Light didn't follow that rule. This part of town was not as flashy as Bourbon Street, but I didn't expect it to be hard to find a bar here. Finally, I spotted a hand-painted sign underneath a flickering light that read, "The Gas Light. 21 and over only."

I pushed open the door expecting to find a small, quiet place. The plain exterior hid a bright, warm interior, filled with noisy patrons sitting at the bar and around tables that occupied the narrow but deep room. In front of me was the end of a long, well-worn wooden bar. It went the length of the entire room and was lined with tall stools. With backpacks, tool belts, and purses slung over each chair, there wasn't an empty seat. Flickering in the cloudy mirror over the back of the bar was the reflection of lights. From shiny brass to black wrought-iron finishes, from porch size to streetlight size, assorted gaslights haphazardly covered the opposite wall.

To the right of the bar was a mix of round and square tables. I was in awe of the server working the room since the tables were packed tightly. With a large tray of full glasses and beer bottles, she maneuvered around like a ballerina. I would have been a bull in a china shop.

"Sammy! You made it," yelled Neal. "Come on back. They don't bite."

"Speak for yourself," said the bald, paint-splattered man seated in the chair I was trying to squeeze behind. His wide, toothless smile caught me off guard while his tablemates snickered.

"I might bite back." I grinned at them, which evidently was the right thing to say as I believe they offered me a drink, a hand in marriage, and a set of dentures. I couldn't quite hear them as Neal steered me over to the table and pulled out a chair for me.

"Glad you found us. I bet you passed by it a few times," Neal said.

"It took a while to find it. Is that on purpose?"

"That's how we like it, hidden from tourists and drunk people. There are enough tourist traps on Bourbon Street. We prefer to keep it just for the neighborhood."

"I can see that," I said as I sipped my Abita beer. This was a place for a local beer and not a syrupy-sweet drink like the famous Hurricane cocktail. I waved off the chipped plastic bowl of peanuts Neal pushed over to me.

"I bet Sissy told you about the peanuts," Neal said. "Did you eat? We could order food in from Frankie's Groceries, or I can call Matt to pick something up on his way here... Well, speak of the devil, here he is."

Headed toward our table could have been Neal's twin with his matching outfit and sandy-brown hair, but that's where the similarities ended. While he smiled as he approached us, he didn't have that outgoing energy Neal had. He frowned as he took the skateboard off the only other chair and handed it to him.

"Sorry, man," Neal said as he placed his skateboard against the wall behind him. "Matt is my roommate, business partner, but more importantly, my best friend. Matt, this is our new neighbor, Sammy."

"I'm Matt Parnell. Nice to meet you," he said as he reached out to shake my hand. "I see Neal is introducing you to the finer parts of our neighborhood. Please tell me you haven't eaten the peanuts."

"No, Sissy warned me." I smiled as I returned his firm handshake. "After running into Frankie, I shopped at her store and filled up on the muffuletta sandwich."

"Her food is great. Everyone in the building shops there, so you'll see her grandson delivering all the time," Matt said.

"I guess he's making deliveries, but I bet he has a thing for Sissy. Or maybe he likes older women like Ruby." Neal laughed while Matt raised his eyebrows at him.

"Ruby? Are you talking about my next-door neighbor?" I asked.

"You've met her already?" Neal said. "I suppose she told you about your negative aura. Or did she tell you to respect her since she's lived in the building longer than anyone else?"

"Yes, to both. Also, that I either brought trouble or invited it in. That was a first. She didn't even mention her name. Or her cats' names." I gave a half-hearted laugh. "I have a feeling I'll like the cats more than her."

"We all do except Matt. Ruby and Matt like each other. He has the brightest aura of us all."

Matt shook his head. "I got her cats down from the roof once and ever since then she's been kind of nice. I really don't understand how she keeps her business running with the way she treats people."

Neal and Matt filled me in on our neighbor, Ruby Virtue, a tarot card reader and spiritual consultant. Libby said she literally came with the building; the previous owners would only sell to them if they promised to rent to Ruby indefinitely. How long she had lived in Thibodeaux Mansion and her age were mysteries. All anyone knew was that she had her own shop on Decatur Street and that her cats, Cleopatra and Nefertiti, were the loves of her life.

"I gathered that much about her cats. She accused me of trying to poison them with the flowers my old coworkers sent me today."

"She's rude to everyone, so don't take it personally. Even Sissy hasn't gotten her to talk, and everyone talks to Sissy," Neal said.

"Besides Ruby, how do you like your apartment? I know Libby was worried that she overdid the New Orleans theme," Matt said.

"I love it. Libby did a great job, although I found a strange book and key on a shelf," I said. "It seems like a diary, but also like a guidebook for the city. I haven't read it yet, but it claims to have riddles that take you around the neighborhood."

"Can't say I've heard of a guidebook like that, and the key with it is odd. What does it look like?" Matt said.

I described it and both guys shook their heads. At first, Matt thought it might have been an old courtyard gate key, but it was too big and elaborate. I asked them about the unlocked gate. Neal explained that after years of the residents losing their keys, William and Libby left it open.

"I take it no one worries about people trespassing or breaking in the building?"

"Don't worry, we haven't had any problems," Neal answered. "Tourists wander in occasionally, but keep your door locked, especially during Mardi Gras."

"If you're concerned, I can talk to William about it," Matt offered.

"No, that's okay," I said. "It's just different from San Francisco where everyone locks everything."

"Speaking of San Francisco, how did you get from there to here? Did you move for a job?" Neal asked.

"No, I'm trying to decide what I want to do next," I said. "I was an administrative assistant, but I'd love to do something with writing or publishing. I needed a change, so I decided that New Orleans would be a good place to start."

"It's a great place to make changes," Matt agreed. "We started our tour guide business about a year ago after finally admitting we hated our jobs. Our version of a premature midlife crisis, you'd call it."

"Best decision we made," Neal said. "The tour industry is fun, except for the paperwork."

"It's harder running a small business than we imagined, but people seem to like our tours."

"Of course they do! There are a ton of tours in this town, but we know ours is better. We talk about actual history and not that vampire bullshit."

I decided this was not the time to share my love of Anne Rice novels, but ventured to ask, "What tours do you offer? I need to take some since I've only been here once before I moved."

Both guys looked surprised. "Really? That's brave or crazy. I'm not sure which. In any case, here's to Sammy, the adventurer!" Neal said as he raised his beer.

We cheered each other with our bottles, and the table of

my new toothless friend did the same. Neal began telling me about their different tours, but Matt stopped him.

"It'll be easier to give Sammy a brochure tomorrow. I don't think she'll remember the details," Matt said as I tried to stifle a yawn.

"I'm sorry, the traveling today has finally gotten to me," I said as I let a yawn escape. "I'd love a flyer so I can pick which tours I'll take as soon as I've caught up on my sleep."

"I'll drop one by, but you'll want to go on all of them," Neal said. "Don't worry, you get the neighbor discount."

After promising them I could find my way home, I returned Neal's tight squeeze and Matt's gentler hug. Their immediate friendliness was surprising, but I welcomed it. Again, that Southern charm was living up to its reputation. I turned down a nightcap from the now bleary-eyed friend as I passed his table. I looked back to give one more wave to the guys, but they were in such a deep discussion that they didn't see me.

I was thankful for a quick walk home and finding my doorstep empty of an irritated neighbor. Thoughts of attractive Southern gentlemen and mouthwatering new food followed me to sleep. I would have stayed in my happy dreamworld until the morning if it wasn't for the loud and insistent banging on my front door.

5

───────

It was 2:30 a.m. when I sat up to the pounding on my front door. The banging continued as I rushed to my door. I assumed I would hear the words "Fire!" or some other dire warning. Instead, it was the drunken slurring of a man, "Dude! It's too early to be in bed! Time for beer!"

Was it a drunk tourist wandering into the courtyard that Neal mentioned could happen? Mardi Gras was still about a week away, so I knew it wasn't a lost parade goer, especially at this hour. I should have ignored whoever was making a scene outside, but my annoyance finally outweighed my common sense.

I'm not sure who was more surprised, exhausted bed-headed me, or the handsome stranger staggering forward into my doorway as I whipped open the door. Although he towered over me, I pushed him backward into the courtyard.

"I'm not your dude. Please leave."

The brown-haired man spilled his beer on his otherwise clean blue Oxford shirt. He wiped a hand on his jeans after putting his bottle and accompanying six-pack on my outside table. His bloodshot eyes looked me up and down.

"You definitely aren't a dude. Where's Mark?"

Inebriated and observant, what a combination. Instead of shutting the door on him, I answered, "I don't know Mark, but my guess is he lived here before me."

"Right! You're the new renter Mom told me about. Shit. I'm sorry." He reached out to shake my hand. "I'm Connor. My folks own the building."

"I'm Samantha, and yes, I'm new." I returned his handshake, hoping it was only beer on his hand.

"I promise I won't bother you like this again. But since you're awake, how about a drink?"

Connor tried to give me a beer. His sly smile was one I was sure he used drunk or sober. I'd seen that look on enough men in bars in San Francisco; I preferred the toothless but genuine grin of my new friend at The Gas Light.

"Does that really work? I mean, banging on people's doors in the middle of the night asking them to party with you?"

"S-sometimes," he stuttered. "Honest, I'm sorry."

I couldn't tell if it surprised him that I didn't jump at the chance for a beer or that I questioned his methods of getting drinking partners. He appeared less confident as he fidgeted with his hands and shuffled his feet. He took what looked like a trumpet mouthpiece and rolled it back and forth in his hand. He reminded me of Carl from eighth grade who hung out on my front porch for an hour after I repeatedly said no to his request for a date.

Connor was no lovelorn boy, but a drunk grown man. But he was also the son of my landlords. I couldn't hide in the girls' bathroom when I saw him like I did with Carl, so I decided not to let him squirm for long. Although, I had to admit there was something charming about his discomfort on being called out.

"Apology accepted. It's a definite no to the drink tonight. Hopefully, I'll meet you again in the daylight." And with that I gave a quick smile and closed my door.

"Damn," he said. I listened to him pick up the six-pack and stumble away.

I returned to bed irritated by the interruption, but I had to admit even in his drunken state, Connor interested me. Definitely handsome, but also trouble, I bet. I wonder if Ruby thought he was trouble, too. I tossed and turned, thinking about my first day in New Orleans. I drifted back to sleep with thoughts of muffulettas and mysterious men.

IT WAS DISCONCERTING to wake up in a strange bed and more so to wake up in a different place and life. If last night was any indication, New Orleans was full of interesting, fun, and sometimes drunk people. Besides Ruby, I hoped all my neighbors would become friends, even Connor. I still needed to meet the tenant in the front apartment. Would it be another charming man, friendly woman, or rude spiritualist?

Finding that out wasn't my priority; coffee was. I forgot to buy it yesterday, and I didn't function without at least one cup. I threw the diary and key in my little backpack and opened my door to leave.

Fortunately, I looked before I stepped out; otherwise, I would have knocked over an empty beer bottle acting as a vase. I recognized the flowers from the courtyard plants. An apology on the back of a Frankie's Groceries receipt explained the gift:

Sorry about last night. Welcome to the building! Drinks are on me whenever you want. From the guy who's not always a jerk, Connor.

I put it on my kitchen counter next to yesterday's flower delivery. While it looked skimpy compared to the lilies, I liked this bouquet better. I hoped it was a heartfelt gift and not the move of a player. It seemed more sincere than slick, or at least I would believe that until Connor showed me otherwise.

To feed my caffeine addiction, my first stop was a place I already knew, Libby's shop, Artistic Coffee & Creations. I discovered her store during a sudden downpour. I learned that rainstorms can come out of nowhere in Louisiana. I was among the many unprepared tourists who sought shelter in the warm, dry coffee shop. While the others left, its owner charmed me into staying.

Libby was a painter, and the café was a compromise with her husband, the practical accountant. With numerous art galleries in town, and countless artists selling their wares in Jackson Square, William felt his wife needed an added draw and source of income to keep the gallery in business. Ten years later, Artistic Coffee & Creations thrived as a popular café with homemade pastries and a rotating collection of paintings, prints, and photographs. While Libby displayed her work from time to time, she preferred to support her fellow artists.

The comforting smell of ground coffee and warm pastries hit me as I walked in. The door barely closed behind me as the line to order extended all the way to the back. I thought at 10 a.m. there would be a lull in the crowds. Evidently there was never a slow time at Libby's.

The line inched forward quietly unlike the rest of the room, which buzzed with caffeinated energy. Groups of two and three patrons chatted with such animation. Even the customers sitting by themselves, typing away on laptops or phones, seem to do so loudly. Everything and everyone here appeared to be on full blast. Was I jet-lagged? Or was I used to coffee shops where people got their fix and hurried on to their next destination?

Libby's yelling across the room interrupted my thoughts, "Sammy, so good to see you!"

She stepped down from the ladder she needed to hang a painting in the only blank space on the back wall. I called it impressionistic since I couldn't decipher what the artist painted. By the bright purple, green, and gold colors, I assumed it was Mardi Gras themed.

Windows lined the wall to the right. The area in between them featured photographs of Mardi Gras parades. Libby even showcased small sculptures on the shelves behind the coffee-and-pastry counter. I admired Libby's dedication to helping people, but the overwhelming amount of art added to the semi-frenzied atmosphere.

Libby pulled me out of line and gave me a hug. "Did you sleep all right? I understand you already met Neal and Matt! Aren't they darling? And Sissy is the best woman!"

I tried to answer, but she kept on talking. She lowered her voice. "I am so sorry about my son! He really is a good soul, I promise. He's just still finding his way in this world."

"No worries. He left me a note and flowers this morning."

"He did?" she squealed. She let out a little cough and continued with her normal tone. "That's wonderful! Now, you must want breakfast. Sit right down and read the paper while I grab a café au lait and a cranberry scone. "

Before I could protest that I didn't need the scone, Libby dashed off behind the counter. I told myself I would run tomorrow. One more day without exercise wouldn't kill me, I hoped.

I sat at the table and opened the newspaper, paying special attention to local news. It would take a while to figure out where all the different neighborhoods were besides the French Quarter. I read an article about the upcoming parades. The smaller groups, or krewes as they were called here, held their parades first before the big krewes had theirs closer to Mardi Gras.

"There's nothing better than a New Orleans parade," Libby said as she put down my treat and coffee. She pointed to another article on the page. "Oh, that's such a shame about those break-ins in the neighborhood. William added a few more locks to the doors here, but if someone wants in, they're going to get in."

I nodded as I took a bite of the warm scone. My scale would scream at me if I came here every day. "Do you recognize this key and book? I found it on one of my bookshelves yesterday. It looks like someone's diary."

She read the first page and laughed. "Oh my, this character is desperate for romance. The key is lovely, though. You should wear it as a necklace."

Before I could object, she placed the key necklace around my neck. "It's beautiful, but I didn't want to take something that belongs to someone else. I thought your last renter might have left it."

"No, he rented it unfurnished, so I furnished it after he moved. I bought the books from Andrew. He lives in apartment one. He owns a bookstore here in the Quarter, Lagniappe Books."

"What books?" I can't say I'd ever heard the word she pronounced "lan yap."

"Lagniappe. It means a little something extra thrown in. And let me tell you, Andrew is something extra himself, although not everyone knows it. He might know what the book is, but keep the necklace. I paid for it so it's now yours."

Libby grinned as she picked up my empty dishes and sauntered back to the counter where another line of customers had formed while she chatted with me. "It adds a little mystery to you, don't you think?"

I fiddled with the key necklace as I walked out the café door. Did it add "a little mystery to me" as Libby suggested? Maybe it was just the bit of lagniappe I needed to fit in.

6

Needing to burn off my breakfast calories, I walked around the neighborhood. Delivery trucks for restaurants and stores maneuvered down Royal Street, jockeying for a space among the few available parking places. A mix of photo-snapping tourists and cell phone-chatting restaurant servers heading to work filled the sidewalks. A large tour group marching toward me forced me up the steps of the Louisiana Supreme Court building. Instead of going back to the sidewalk, I sat by the statue of Chief Justice Edward White and eavesdropped on the lecture. With his monotone voice and lackluster list of facts, the guide was losing his customers' attention and mine.

It was a perfect time to read more of the diary before I took it to my neighbor's bookstore:

OCTOBER 5TH

Here's the first riddle my beloved gave me:

To house an exiled man was the original purpose of this historical building. Although he never made it here, his spirit lives on in this grocery store turned restaurant. Come have a Pimm's Cup here with me and we'll take in the history with a meal in the alcove. Perhaps we'll leave our mark underneath the table? A heart with our initials will prove we were there....

AFTER A FEW TRIES, I had the answer and we had our first real date. And yes, we left a sign of our love there. It was an incredible evening and I can't wait to learn more about New Orleans and my new beau.

BEFORE I COULD TURN the page, I answered my cell phone to hear, "He's not getting another sponge bath! Tell him we're not a spa. Cheeky old man.... Hey, Sammy! Sorry about that. I'm at work now, but I thought we could have dinner tonight. Oh, this is Sissy, your neighbor. Hope you don't mind that Libby gave me your number."

There was no doubt it was Sissy, the minute she spoke. Her thick Southern accent and quick manner of speaking was distinctive. "Hi! I guessed it was you. I'd love to meet."

"Great! I could pick a place, but I figure you have restaurants you want to try."

"Actually, I do." I opened the diary. "I found this riddle, and I think I know the answer." After reading the entry, I asked, "It's Napoleon House, right?"

"You got it! We'll make a local out of you quick as can be. I need to run, but I'll meet you there at 7 p.m. I don't care if he's begging, he's not getting a foot rub. Girl, you need to be a stronger woman and nurse..." I giggled as I ended the call, betting Sissy was about to enforce a few rules on the unsuspecting "cheeky old man."

Another tour group positioned themselves next to me,

so I put the diary away. I searched for Lagniappe Books on my phone so I wouldn't miss it like The Gas Light, but it wasn't necessary. I would have found it even without the address.

With their faded façades and crumbling brick stairs, many small stores along Royal Street appear closed even when they're open. Andrew's business was different. In the middle of a bright white building, with its doors and windows flanked by glossy black shutters, the shop was easy to find. Engraved on a polished brass plate was "Lagniappe Books, Established 2006." I went up the solid stairs to the entrance, expecting a small store with overflowing shelves and little room to walk. Like my expectations of The Gas Light, I was wrong again.

Tall, gleaming mahogany shelves lined the right and left walls similar to other bookstores. The back of the store, however, resembled a sitting room with a burgundy love seat and two matching chairs surrounding a low marble-topped coffee table. It was as if I were in someone's personal library. I assumed the long dining table, covered in neatly stacked books and a laptop, in the center of the room, doubled as a sales counter with its lone chair positioned at the end.

The combination of a cozy living room and the library atmosphere made this store different from other bookstores. It was a place to respect books, but also to sit and discuss them. Pride of ownership was obvious from the design to the organization of the books to the cleanliness of the shop. Would the owner match his store?

I was alone until a door behind the seating area opened. A man immediately greeted me: "Samantha, I'm so pleased you came to my shop. I'm Andrew Ballard, your neighbor and proprietor of Lagniappe Books."

Startled, I didn't reply, but took in the man in front of me. He was the embodiment of his store. His clothes mimicked the formality of the space with his white button-down shirt, topped off with a bright red bow tie and khaki pants. His face, however, reflected the warmth of the store with a slight dimple appearing as he gave a wide smile. I placed him in his late forties or early fifties with his cropped salt-and-pepper hair.

"I'm sorry, did I surprise you? Libby told me you moved in, and as the tenant of the front apartment, I know many of the comings and goings of our little community."

Hopefully, I didn't appear rude as I looked into his pale blue eyes as he shook my hand. Never had I met anyone whose eyes were so light, and I couldn't help but stare at them. The seriousness of his eyes in contrast to his friendly smile made him mysteriously handsome.

"Yes, you did, but I'm learning that everyone knows everybody here," I said after I stopped gawking at him. "What a beautiful store. You have books on every subject." I wandered past the bookshelves leading to the back of the shop. I moved from a shelf labeled "Southern Fiction" to another titled "Voodoo."

"I try to offer books on as many subjects as I can. You've found the Voodoo section. One of my personal interests."

I thought I didn't react outwardly, but I must have since Andrew let out a low laugh. Humorous or sinister, I couldn't tell. "I assume your knowledge of Voodoo is limited to the tourist version they spew on tours and in tacky gift shops."

"Guilty as charged." I smiled as I moved past the section. "I do understand it's actually a religion and not a blood-sacrificing cult." At least I hoped I was right as Andrew stared at me a little more intensely.

"You are correct. Here, please take my book. To get a better understanding of the subject."

The front cover featured the title *Voodoo: A Historical Perspective.* "Thank you very much. I look forward to reading it. And speaking of books, I have one to ask you about." I took the diary out of my backpack and handed it to him.

"I found it on a bookshelf in my apartment. Libby said it might have come in the box she bought from you."

After scanning a few pages, a surprising snort came out of Andrew. "This diary is a bit tawdry, isn't it? I buy books from estate sales, but I don't recognize it." He gave the journal back. "I'm not sure it's worth reading."

"I must admit, I love riddles and scavenger hunts, so I'll give the book a try and see what I find. But there was a key with it." I took the necklace off, placing it on the table. "Libby insisted I wear it, but I won't take it if it belongs to you."

"Samantha, you've saved the best for last. What an exquisite key!" He inspected it for a moment. "It is an antique, but what does it open? May I photograph it? With a little research I am sure I can find the answer. Why don't I copy the diary just in case it has something to do with the key?" As I nodded yes, he hurried to his back room and copied them.

While he was busy, I looked throughout the shelves and found *Dinner at Antoine's* by Frances Parkinson Keyes.

"A good choice for a newcomer to New Orleans," Andrew said as he returned the diary and key. "Do you like mysteries?"

"I've loved them since I started reading," I said as I put the book on the table and got out my wallet to pay. "I enjoy stories about New Orleans, and if there's a mystery in it, even better."

"You are a woman who knows what she wants."

"With books, at least. I'm still deciding what I want to be when I grow up."

"That is the story of many newcomers to the city. Many are searching for something new or something missing."

"That sounds like me." I laughed. "Glad I'm not alone."

"No, please take that book along with my own," he said as I tried to hand him my credit card. "Think of them as my version of a housewarming gift. I don't make casseroles, and I'm positive Sissy brought you a fruit basket."

"Yes, she did, and Matt and Neal took me out for drinks."

"And Connor left flowers."

"You do know what goes on in the building."

"The only thing I don't know is if you met Ruby. If you have, ignore most of what she says." He winked. "Many of her readings are wrong."

"I'm glad to hear that she's not perfect with her spiritual predictions."

"She means well, but I keep my distance from her. She acts as if she prefers it that way."

"I can believe that. Are you sure I can't buy the book from you?"

"No, you cannot. I hope you'll come by the store again. I enjoyed meeting you. Don't forget your key."

He placed the necklace around my neck. "I agree with Libby that this belongs to you. It suits you," he said with a wide smile. "This might be the key to your future."

His sincerity surprised me. The door opening and a flock of elderly ladies streaming into the shop shattered the moment.

"Mr. Andrew, we're here for our lecture," announced the apparent leader of the group as they hurried to the seating area.

"Hello, Miss Margaret. I'll be with you in a minute."

He pointed toward the back as the chatty women walked past us. "I give lectures to groups on many historical topics. Today is the Battle of New Orleans. You're welcome to join them."

Although Andrew invited me to the lesson, the glare from the ladies told me they did not. Not wanting to provoke the women's wrath, I declined his offer. Now, if it had been about Voodoo, I would have squeezed onto the love seat with them.

"Another time I would love to," I said as I gathered my books. "I'm meeting Sissy for dinner tonight, and I need to get a few things done beforehand."

"Join us anytime," he replied. "You two will have much to discuss. She's full of local knowledge and is such a delightful person. Let me know what you think of my book and Voodoo."

I left the shop with the diary, my books, and what was now my key around my neck. Curiosity about my new neighbor came along with me, too. Andrew was "a little something extra" just like Libby said.

7

With my arms full of books, I skipped coffee shopping. And now I had an excuse to stop by Libby's café for breakfast tomorrow. Damn those scones. As I walked up to my door, I spotted a shiny pink bag sitting on the doormat. Another gift?

After putting my things down on my courtyard table, I picked up the lightweight bag. A typewritten note of "Welcome Home" was on the attached gift card. I pulled out layers of silver tissue paper to find a doll. With her gingerbread shape, hand-stitched face, and brown yarn pigtailed hair, she appeared a simple toy at first. The pink and white smocked gingham dress added a surprising realistic touch. The craftsmanship and sweet details gave her a charm that mass-market dolls lacked. I flipped her over and lifted the dress, already knowing I would discover the initials "BB" on her backside.

I knew this doll.

After gathering my bags and fumbling for my key, I opened the door and rushed inside to the shelf with my childhood collection of Nancy Drew books. In front of them sat my only doll. I turned her over and even through the water stains, the "BB" stitched on my doll's behind was easy to see. Not only did she have the same initials as my new gift, but my original one had the same dress and pigtails.

I sank into my love seat with both dolls in my hand. I always assumed mine was one of a kind. I double-checked the bag, but didn't find another card. Such a strange present to give, and what was the chance it would be the same doll I already own?

Few people knew I had her. In my San Francisco apartment, I kept her on a shelf in my bedroom, so only a handful of visitors ever saw her. The last man who shared my bed was not the type to send a doll. Or any gift for that matter.

If this doll didn't match my own, I'd say it was for someone else. The only person who had anything to do with toys these days was my friend Madeline in San Francisco, so I called her. She denied sending it.

"Samantha, Athena would kill me if I sent you one of her dolls. I'm happy to send her to you if you'd prefer a real tantrum-throwing toddler."

I forgot about the strange gift as Madeline rambled about the trials and tribulations of her daughter's terrible-twos stage. After she finished her stories, I filled her in on my new life so far. I impressed her with my progress, and she insisted on more pictures of the men I'd met. In the meantime, she said she would find them on Facebook. "Married momma needs a hobby," she said as she promised not to embarrass me online.

Ending the call made me homesick for my friend, but my dinner with Sissy was the perfect remedy. I spotted Napoleon House with its bicorn hat sign and name spelled out in tiles in front of the entryway. With its gray exterior walls, the wrought-iron balcony on its second floor gave it a bit more character, but it wasn't until I walked in that it impressed me with its history. The same peeling plaster walls continued throughout the room, but they were covered with paintings, news clippings, and graffiti-like signatures. I peered into the courtyard with tables full of patrons.

I arrived earlier than Sissy so I could take the place in and enjoy my first Pimm's cup, the signature drink of the restaurant. The bartender repeatedly filled glasses with lemonade, Pimm's liqueur, which I learned was gin based, a splash of 7UP, and garnished them with a cucumber slice. It was light, refreshing, and a New Orleans classic. Just what I'd like to be some day, I laughed to myself. I needed to add a drink section to my sandwich blog idea.

"Sammy! You started without me, naughty girl!" Strong arms smelling of antiseptic wrapped around my shoulders. Did anyone make a subtle entrance in this town?

I turned and hugged Sissy back. "Sorry, I couldn't help myself. Mike, can you please get my friend a drink?"

"First name with the bartender already? I like your style. Thanks, Mike." He had started the Pimm's cup for her even before I asked. Sissy must be friendly with everyone in the Quarter.

"I hope you don't mind waiting at the bar for a bit," I said. "I asked the hostess for the table in the alcove."

"Of course not," Sissy replied. "It's the perfect spot, and you should sit there for your first time here."

We waited for just a few minutes for the table to open up. The hostess greeted Sissy with a hug before seating us. After ordering muffulettas with a side of jambalaya, we chatted nonstop. She was easy to talk to, and we discovered we had much in common, including mystery books, running, and British TV shows. I had assumed she'd grown up in New Orleans, but her hometown was Metairie, a suburb of the city. After graduating from Louisiana State University (LSU), she moved into the French Quarter.

"I just love it here. Once you discover the streets and restaurants outside the tourist areas, you'll love the city even more. My family keeps begging me to come back home, but I don't want to settle down like my brothers."

Sissy filled me in on her three brothers with their "gaggle of cutie-pie children" as she called them. Her parents doted on their grandchildren, and although they already had nine, they wanted even more. "How about you? Brothers or sisters? Where's your family?"

This was always the awkward part of the "getting to know you process" for me. Sometimes it ended the conversation or made people pity me. I didn't want either to happen with Sissy.

"Well, the short story is that I became an orphan when I was about two after Hurricane Geoffrey. My parents, who lived in Baton Rouge, adopted me. We moved to Florida a few months later, so I grew up there until I left for college in San Francisco. They died in a car accident over a year ago so it's just me."

Sissy's response was neither pity nor an awkward pause in the conversation. "Wow, Sammy, I'm so sorry. No siblings, then? Well, you can have some of mine!" She laughed and held my hand while giving it a quick squeeze. "So, you might be a Louisianan! What about your birth family?"

"The police found me on the side of I-10. They assumed my parents must have been driving to safety, and we got caught up in the storm."

Sissy signaled our waiter for another round of drinks and then said, "I can't even imagine what it was like for you. You don't know anything about what happened to you?"

"No one claimed me, so I went into foster care, and I was fortunate that my parents adopted me."

"They sound like good people, but you haven't searched out to your biological family? Now that you're here, will you?" Sissy nodded to the waiter who brought the next round of drinks, and continued, "Is that the reason you moved to New Orleans?"

"Actually, I came here for a change. I turned thirty and felt like I was going nowhere."

"Oh, I hear you. I turned thirty last year and panicked for a quick moment. A weekend of babysitting my nieces and nephews cured me."

We laughed, but Sissy hadn't forgotten her original question. "Let's get back to your other reason for moving here. Come on, it must be to find your birth family."

I took a long sip of my drink, deciding what to say next. Only my friend Madeline knew this part of my story. Looking into Sissy's kind eyes, my heart told me to trust her.

"Yes, it is."

"I knew it! What do you know so far?"

"Just this." I opened my backpack and pulled out my wallet where tucked inside was a snapshot. I handed it to Sissy who unfolded it.

"This is you, isn't it? It's a bit faded, but there's no denying that's your red hair and that smattering of freckles on your nose."

The toddler in the picture was sitting on a chair, both covered in what appeared to be powdered sugar. On the table was a plate of beignets, the square doughnut-like fried confection that were always coated in messy powdered sugar. The girl was clutching one in her hand and grinning from ear to ear.

"I think so, and I think it was taken at Café du Monde."

Sissy looked over every inch of the photo, inspecting it as if it were a piece of fine art. "I agree. You can see the café's menu on the napkin dispenser. No other beignet place has that same menu or puts up with that much powdered sugar everywhere. What's the mystery behind the picture?"

"After my parents passed away, I found it in my mother's desk hidden underneath a pile of old papers. She never showed it to me."

"Why would she hide it?" Sissy asked. "They could have brought you here before you moved to Florida. Café du Monde is a tradition for Louisiana families and tourists alike."

"Look at the date on the back."

"It says May 1990. Oh. Now I understand."

"Yes, it's three months before the hurricane. My parents didn't take that photo. At least not my adoptive parents."

We sat in silence. I could tell that Sissy was processing what I had learned just over a year ago. My mom and dad had some information about me pre-hurricane and never showed it to me. I tried not to let my confusion and anger about my parents' actions, or lack thereof, taint my memories of them. This was why I had only told Madeline, and now Sissy, about this.

"Was there anything else with it?" Sissy asked as she placed the photo in my hand.

"Nothing. This was it. That's all I have to go on."

"Are you sure you want to find out? There could be a good reason they hid this."

"I've thought that, too," I said as I put the picture away. "My parents were kind people, so I'd like to give them the benefit of the doubt."

"You have a lot to think about, but whatever you do, I'm here to help." Sissy smiled and gave my hand a quick squeeze before releasing it. I forgot she was holding it as I let myself get wrapped up in our conversation. She was right; researching my past was a big undertaking, and at times, I wasn't sure if I was ready for what I might find.

"Let's forget my past and talk about this stranger's story." I grabbed the diary out of my backpack. "Here's where I found that riddle about Napoleon House. It's a journal I discovered in my apartment. This will make you laugh!"

Sissy took the book and giggled after reading the restaurant entry. "Oh my, it's like a terrible romance novel, isn't it? Let's see if we can find this heart they supposedly left."

We looked at all the names and initials that filled every inch of the plaster walls around us. The tradition of leaving your name must have started decades ago, as there wasn't an empty spot. I pushed back my chair and sat on the floor to search for the heart.

"Sammy, are you okay? How many Pimm's cups did you have before I got here?"

"The diary said they put their initials under the table. I haven't had that much to drink!"

"Thank goodness! I'm glad you're not a lightweight or a lush," she said as she joined me under her side of the table.

When the waiter came over, he didn't bat an eyelash at us. "Do you need a pen to write your names on the wall?"

"No, honey, we're good. Mine is over by the bar. Hold it, Sammy, your name isn't here yet. I guess we need that pen."

I stuck my head up and took the pen from the grinning waiter. "Thanks."

"Glad to help, but y'all shouldn't sit too long on that floor. I'll bring towels over to wipe your hands."

Sissy and I both looked at the floor and realized it wasn't the cleanest place to be sitting. I scribbled my name on the wall as "Sammy" instead of "Samantha" since it seemed more appropriate.

We took the damp bar towels from our waiter, and then we compared notes. Most of the writing were individual names, but we found four hearts: "N + A," "C+S," "S + K," and "J +D." I jotted the initials down in a small notebook I always carried with me.

"That was fun! Keep me posted about your search for your family and the diary. Hold on, I got a text," Sissy said as we walked outside the restaurant at the end of our meal. "It's Neal telling us to come to The Gas Light."

"I'm tired, but I could go for one drink. How about you?"

"I'd love to, but I promised my boyfriend I would go over to his place tonight. Our schedules keep us apart most of the time, so I need to see him when I can," Sissy replied as she hugged me goodbye. "Say hi to the boys. We'll do this again real soon."

I walked toward the bar with a spring in my step. It wasn't just the alcohol that put me in a lighthearted mood. Sissy was a keeper. It took a while to make good friends in San Francisco, so I couldn't believe my luck in finding her. Or I guess she found me. Whatever the case was, I was thankful for her friendship already. As I strolled up to The Gas Light, it looked as if Neal and Matt didn't feel the same way about their relationship.

8

———————

Neal and Matt's tense expressions and angry voices were a sharp contrast to last night's relaxed faces and jovial manner. They were facing each other with little space in between them which concerned me that the exchange would turn physical. As their words grew louder, I turned to retreat. I only made it a few steps when Neal yelled, "Sammy! Hey, sorry, we were discussing work. You ready for a drink?"

I walked toward them while Matt whispered under his breath to Neal. I couldn't make out Neal's response, but from Matt's long sigh, I gathered it wasn't what he wanted to hear. Whatever they argued about, they put it aside as we went into the bar.

Several people entered The Gas Light during their disagreement, so I was curious if anyone would say anything. The bartender raised a pierced eyebrow at us, but no one commented until I heard a thick Southern accent call out, "Another business fight, or did one of y'all forget to replace the toilet paper again?"

The speaker was a man who looked like he could be

Neal's older brother with his messy brown hair obscuring his eyes and a crooked grin. He towered over Neal as they performed an elaborate handshake.

"Joey, we never replace the toilet paper unless we're entertaining," Neal said.

Joey shook Matt's hand in the traditional manner. I wasn't surprised as Matt didn't strike me as someone who followed "the bro code" as my male friends back in San Francisco called it. I wondered which handshake I would get when Joey turned in my direction.

"And who is this? Are you trying to convince her to take one of your tours? I wouldn't bother since the guys don't dress as vampires or pirates." Joey shook my hand and winked.

"But they promised me they did." I laughed as I rested on the barstool that Matt offered me. He sat next to me as Joey and Neal stood behind us. "I guess I'll have to find another tour."

"If you really want a pirate or vampire, I might have a costume," Neal replied.

"I bet you do. Hi, I'm Joey Martin. How did you end up with these two, miss?"

"I'm Samantha Richardson. I just moved into the same building as Matt and Neal."

The bartender interrupted us by placing four bottles of Abita beer on the bar. "I assumed the usual, guys. And since you're with them, I guessed you'd have what they're having. Am I wrong?" Her firm voice told me not to tell her then, or ever, that she was mistaken. The heavy rings that lined her fingers looked like she wore brass knuckles, but her pale yellow sweater and twinkling eyes softened her personality.

"Yes, I'll take a beer, thanks."

"Good. Terry sent it over. He said you're all right." She

pointed over to last night's toothless new friend who raised his bottle so I did the same in return. "He doesn't like many people, so you must be okay. Even if you're hanging out with these guys."

"Oh, come on, Rose, you know you love us," Neal said as he leaned over the bar and kissed her on the cheek. "We're your favorites, besides Terry."

To my surprise, she blushed. "You think you're everyone's favorite." She turned and put out her hand. "Hi, Sammy, I'm Rose. Neal's head is big enough, so don't let him know that he's right."

"Great to meet you. I'll keep your secret safe," I said as I tried not to wince as I removed my hand from her grip. Her name may be delicate, but Rose was no weeping willow even if she had a soft spot for Neal.

"Actually, I adore Matt the most, but Joey might be a close second," Rose teased as she headed off to the other side of the bar.

"See, I told you she liked you." Neal slapped Matt on his back. "Joey, you might have a chance, too."

"Hilarious. I'm just glad we're allowed in after the skateboard incident," Matt said.

"Dare I ask?"

To their loud interjections, Matt told me how a late night of drinking led Neal and Joey to attempt to race their skateboards around the bar. Rose put a quick stop to it when they tried to climb on top of the bar for a jumping competition. They both landed on their butts and almost hit their heads as Rose grabbed their skateboards from underneath them.

"I was bruised and hungover for days," Joey lamented.

"No wonder. You're a bit too old to be riding a skateboard, aren't you?" Matt asked.

"Age is just a number," Joey said, seemingly not offended

by what I took to be an insult by Matt. "You act like you're older than me, Matt."

"If you mean I'm a responsible thirty-year-old business owner and not a thirty-eight-year-old perpetual grad student, then yes, I act older than you," Matt said.

Joey laughed off Matt's obvious insult. "Touché, my friend."

"Okay, enough, you two; we don't want Sammy to think we fight all the time," Neal said.

Joey's cell phone rang. "Sorry, got to get this. I'll be right back." He headed to the door after giving Neal a high five.

"Man, you always give him a hard time," Neal said to Matt. "He's trying to be friendly."

"Yeah, I get it." Matt sighed. "He's been over a lot and I need some space. Sorry, Sammy, I hope I didn't come across as a jerk or make you think Joey is one. He's okay."

"How do you know Joey? He's not a college friend, what with the age difference, I assume."

"We met him after he moved to New Orleans. He was here one night, and we hit it off. He's a good guy. Not as good as me." Neal grinned as he raised his empty bottle in Rose's direction. "Need another?"

I looked at my half-drunk beer and shook my head. "It seems easy to make friends around here."

Rose came over with Neal's drink. "People are friendly here, but they come and go. I hope these boys stay, though. They pay for their drinks, unlike other people we know."

"She must mean Connor." Matt frowned as he pulled out money for the round of beers. I insisted Rose take my credit card to start a tab, much to the guys' objections.

"Hopefully it wasn't about Joey," Neal said. When Rose returned, he asked her, "Were you talking about Joey?"

"No, he's slipped a few times, but he always pays the next

day. Students are usually good about paying for themselves. Restaurant managers are another story…"

"Connor," the roommates said in unison.

"Have you met him yet? Being charming and Libby's son means he gets away with a lot," Matt said.

"Oh, he's not bad. He's just cocky, and that's annoying, when we like the same woman," Neal said to Rose. She smiled and returned to the other end of the bar.

I told the story of meeting Connor, and they found it amusing but not surprising. He had a reputation for trying to get someone, if not the whole building, to party with him after he finished working. He was a manager at a popular Bourbon Street restaurant. He might be confident, but it sounded like Connor was good at his job at least.

"Well, as long as he doesn't bang on my door in the middle of the night, again, I'm willing to give him another chance."

"Looks like you have a chance now," Matt said as he nodded toward the opening door.

My drunken visitor sauntered up to the bar, but stopped short when he saw our group. His swagger disappeared as he stared at me. Was he surprised, or was he afraid I would reprimand him for last night's interruption? No one spoke for a moment, so I took charge.

"Hi, Connor. I'm Samantha from last night." I reached out to shake his hand. "Nice to meet you when I'm awake."

He laughed as he shook my hand. "Okay, I deserved that. I'm sorry about it, really. Did you get my flowers?"

"I did, thank you."

"Good. I owe you a drink. Can I buy you another beer?"

"I started a tab already, so next time," I said. "Can I get you one?"

Rose placed a beer in front of Connor. "Here's your usual. Now about your tab…"

Connor's eyes widened as he looked at the paper Rose gave him, but he took several twenties out of his wallet. He pushed the note and money toward her and seemed to regain his composure. "Thanks. The rest is for you and the other bartenders. I won't let it happen again."

"No, *I* won't let it happen again," Rose said with a smile on her face, but not with her voice. "I think we understand each other."

"Loud and clear," Connor said quietly, but then smiled and turned to Matt and Neal. "How's business? It looked like y'all were busy when you passed the restaurant yesterday."

"It's picking up now that Mardi Gras is almost here," Neal said. "Thanks for sending that group the other day."

"Yeah, thanks," Matt agreed, but it seemed half-hearted. What had Connor done to annoy him? Perhaps it was just his personality that rubbed him the wrong way.

Joey reentered the bar and signaled Rose for a drink. "Hey, Connor. Sorry about that. I have a love slash hate relationship with this damn phone."

"That reminds me; I need your number, Sammy. I had to text Sissy to invite you here," Neal said as he pulled out his phone. "Actually, just give me yours and I'll enter my info in."

I took my phone out from my bag and handed it to Neal. "Could I get everyone's number? If you don't mind."

Neal, Matt, and Connor entered their information into my contacts. Joey went last and apologized for his slow typing skills. The rest of us had a thorough discussion about the importance of social media for businesses.

"Okay, you've sold me on adding an Instagram account

for the business. I'll set it up because if I let Neal take photos, they might be obscene," Matt said.

"Who, me?" Neal asked.

"Yes, you!" we all shouted at once. The joking continued as Neal took off his shirt and showed his supposed modeling skills. When the table of construction workers paid him ten dollars to put his clothes back on, he stopped. I used the napkin Rose handed me to wipe my eyes from laughing.

"Neal, you are crazy," Connor said. "Sammy, are you sure you want to live in our building with this nut?"

"Oh, I've seen worse," I answered after shaking my head to Rose's offer of another drink. "Now if Neal goes around dressed as a vampire, I may leave."

"You wound me, my lady," Neal said as he clutched his chest and staggered backward. "And to think I was going to suggest we have a party to welcome you to the building."

"That's a great idea," Matt said. "Connor, can you arrange it with your mom?"

"I'll set it up. You know my momma can't resist throwing a party."

"I hope you'll invite me even though I'm just a poor friend living in the outskirts of the quarter," Joey said.

"Of course," Neal said while slapping Joey on the back. "You're part of the family."

"And you're with us enough, it's like you live there," Matt added.

"Thanks, guys," Joey said. "See, Sammy, you've landed in the right place."

"I couldn't agree more," I replied. I went to ask Rose for my check, but she already had it in her hand. "You can read minds, Rose."

"A good bartender can read people, but from your empty

bottle to the yawn you keep stifling, it was an easy guess you're calling it a night."

"Rose knows all," Matt said as he got up from his barstool. "Sammy, I'm ready to go home, too. And so are you, Neal. We have a private tour at 9 a.m."

Neal chugged the last of his beer and put the bottle down. Joey did the same.

"Okay, dad," Neal said.

"Neal..."

"Just joking, Matt. Let's head out."

"Hey, I left my sweatshirt at your place the other day," Joey said. "Mind if I grab it now?"

"Sure, come back with us," Neal said.

"I'll leave with you, too," Connor said as he followed us toward the door. "Thanks, Rose."

"You're welcome," she said. "See y'all soon, including you, Sammy."

I waved goodbye to her and my new friend Terry, who gave me a toothless grin back.

Connor walked by my side, and we casually talked about generic subjects like the weather. I thought he wanted to ask more, but Joey interrupted our conversation to ask about Connor's restaurant. I fell back to join Neal and Matt to ask them about their private tour the next day. I smiled every time Connor glanced at me, but neither of us could find a break to speak to one another. And our chatting friends didn't seem to catch on that we wanted to talk to each other.

We entered the courtyard and stood by the staircase that led up to the second floor where Neal and Matt lived. After a few minutes of talking, we heard a door open and bang close.

"That's Ruby's sign to be quiet," Matt said as he headed up the stairs.

"Y'all have got the strangest neighbor," Joey said as he followed behind Neal. "She's weirder than my grandmother and that's saying a lot."

They left Connor and me in the courtyard. Finally alone, I started to ask him about the trumpet mouthpiece he was twirling in his hand then, like he did the first night I met him. I didn't get the chance as he answered a call. "Hi, Momma. I just got home. I'll come and see you."

He mouthed good night and continued to talk to her as he opened the door that led into the main building. Now I knew who lived where in the main house: Connor lived on the top floor, while his parents were on the second floor and Andrew was on the first floor.

Now I had met everyone in Thibodeaux Mansion and with meeting Joey, Frankie, and Frank, my circle of friends was already pretty wide for two days in a new city. As I finally settled down to sleep, I hoped my search for my past would go as smoothly as the start of my future.

9

———

The next morning my cell phone woke me with its constant dinging. I forgot to turn off notifications, but I didn't expect communications this early. Three text messages glared at me from Madeline. The first was just *Hello.* The second said *No updates online. Where are they?* The final was *Don't keep me hanging.*

It was only 6 a.m. in California so she must be up with her daughter. A trip to Café du Monde would solve my lack of coffee in the house and fulfill my friend's desire for touristy pictures. More importantly, I would see where my mysterious childhood photo was taken.

On my first visit to New Orleans, I avoided the café. The amateur detective in me wanted to go there, but the woman orphaned twice in a lifetime feared what she might find. After talking with Sissy last night, I had the courage to face whatever I would discover there.

By the time I got dressed and made it to the iconic café, a long line had already formed to get a table. As I waited, I looked at the spot from the photo. Hoping to remember something or feel something, I stared at the area.

Nothing happened.

I closed my eyes so I could concentrate on the sounds of the restaurant. The murmuring of voices, the clanking of dishes, and the wisps of music from outside the café didn't spark any flashbacks. Even inhaling the scents of sweet beignets and bitter chicory coffee didn't evoke any memories.

Disappointed and frustrated, I left the line and ordered from the take-out counter.

After I got my breakfast, I snapped a selfie in front of the menu posted on the wall and sent it to Madeline. Her response, *Finally! Enjoy,* made me smile. It also reminded me it was all right to focus on my current life in New Orleans and not my past, at least for a bit.

I crossed the road to Jackson Square. It's the most recognizable landmark in the neighborhood, besides Bourbon Street. Most people visit it to take a picture in front of the statue of General Andrew Jackson. Others use the park as a place to walk, sit on the grass, or eat beignets as evidenced by the piles of powdered sugar on the ground by the benches.

I found a bench all to myself, which was a lucky find on a beautiful morning. It was a cool day in that I needed a light jacket over my long-sleeved shirt, but the sun was shining. The bouncy songs from the brass band playing in front of The Presbytère floated over the wrought-iron fence surrounding the park. I tapped my toes along to the music as I sipped my sharp chicory coffee and devoured the sweet and fluffy beignets. Where else but New Orleans could I have a decadent breakfast while listening to incredible musicians under a clear blue sky?

From my spot I saw The Presbytère, St. Louis Cathedral, and the Cabildo. I loved how the city preserved so many of their historic buildings. While it was an obstacle course maneuvering through scaffolding and closed sidewalks, I didn't mind it if it meant the character and the stories of the Quarter were being protected.

Thinking of history reminded me I hadn't read the next entry in the diary.

OCTOBER 7TH

The romantic journey continued with another clue:

The match to the Cabildo, this stately building is full of history. From monks to businesses, from a courthouse to a museum, this place holds two exhibits of opposite events. From life to death, we'll learn more about our city of extremes. Let's mark our life with our initials while we view the parade...

We had a spectacular time pretending we were somewhere else, but our love is not a fantasy. It's real. How lucky am I to have this man in my life in the most incredible city?

THE PRESBYTÈRE WAS THERE WAITING for me to follow the next clue.

After paying for my ticket, I ignored the Hurricane Katrina section and rushed up the stairs. On my first visit to New Orleans, I had enough time to go through that exhibit and I wasn't ready to see it again. While showing the strength and resilience of the city, the show broke my heart.

For weeks after, when I put on my pants, I thought of a pair of jeans on display. A man wrote his name, social security number, and his wife's phone number so they could identify him if he died. When I told that story to my San Francisco friends, they questioned my sanity about moving to a place known for hurricanes. I would respond, "One

word: earthquakes." Every part of the country was suscep-
tible to natural disasters. As an orphan of a hurricane, I
hoped I'd lived through the worst.

The "life" exhibit, as the diary referred to it, covered the
origin of Mardi Gras, the krewes, and the celebrations. I
wanted to see all the rooms, but my curiosity got the best of
me and I headed straight to the parade area. The main
attraction was a float.

Although it was big, I could tell this wasn't an actual
parade float. According to the pictures on the wall, the real
one would take up the entire room, if not more. The replica
still impressed me with its decorations of ceiling-grazing
palm trees surrounded by oversized vibrant flowers. The
New Orleans Police Department's (NOPD) metal barriers in
front added to its authenticity. As I snapped a few photos for
Instagram, I noticed an arrow pointing toward the back. I
followed it to find stairs leading behind the façade.

After walking up the steps, I became a participant in a
parade. Okay, pretend one, but I couldn't help but laugh
watching a film of people along a street calling out for beads
and trinkets. Parents held their children up on their shoulders to grab the "throws." Kids and adults alike ran beside
the float as it slowly advanced down the road. Amazing how
a display and a video made me feel like I was at the parade. I
would ask Sissy if she belonged to a krewe.

After the film started up again, I remembered my real
purpose here, the diary. Time to discover if any initials were
here. No graffiti on the back wall or on the video screen wall.
Last, I checked the safety railing protecting the screen.

At first, the bar appeared unblemished, but as I slid my
hand underneath it, from left to right, the underside became
rough and uneven. Crouching down on my knees, I saw a
few names crudely carved into the rail. I was just about to

stand up when my eye caught one heart with the initials "S + K" in a heart etched into the final inch of the bar.

I opened my notebook to go over my finds from Napoleon House, and sure enough "S + K" was a set of the initials I jotted down. This could be a coincidence, but it seemed odd, since there were no other hearts on the bar. Two for two on the diary. I still didn't know if the journal was real or just an unusual guide book.

I started to check the next diary entry, but a man and a little boy bounded up the stairs. I left them so they could enjoy the display by themselves. The boy's giggles proved I wasn't the only one who enjoyed the fake parade.

It was strangely quiet in the other rooms, so my ears perked up when I heard footsteps behind me. I turned around expecting to find the father and son from the float room, but no one was there.

I continued into a corridor lined with what appeared to be porta-potties. I pulled on a door to find they were just the fake fronts; I noted the women's and men's signs above two of the doors. I loved New Orleans' quirky sense of humor. I walked farther into the bathroom hallway and once again felt someone's presence. I slowed my pace and then abruptly turned, expecting to face the person following me.

No one was there.

I opened the women's restroom door and stopped a few steps inside. My heart beat faster and goose bumps shot up on my arms. Why am I so paranoid? I waited a minute and once again heard footsteps. The sound echoed through the corridor and the pace picked up the closer it got.

I was being followed.

Frantically throwing open the door, I confronted my stalker. Instead, I came face-to-face with a frazzled-looking woman holding a foul-smelling infant.

"Oh, I'm so sorry," I said as I sidestepped the confused mother.

"Rude or drunk?" she muttered under her breath as I held the door open for her.

I didn't make eye contact with her as I tried to walk casually out of the bathroom, but stumbled over my own feet. I glanced up and down the hall; it was empty.

No, just stupid.

10

———

I left the museum feeling like an idiot. Why would anybody be following me? Everyone I'd met so far would say hi instead of pursuing me down a corridor of porta-potties. At least I gave the irritated mom a good story to share. I headed to Frankie's for lunch as the crowds in the area had exploded since the morning.

Opening the door to the store, a smell assaulted me. Was something burning?

"Don't worry, Nonna is making the roux." Frank grinned. "It's a mix of oil and flour, and to make it right, you almost burn it. By your face, my guess is you haven't made gumbo."

"True dat. Is that how you say it?"

"You're already settling in, Sammy, if you're using our slang. You didn't say it in California." He sauntered over next to me.

"Definitely not," I said. "How do you know where I'm from? Is it that obvious?"

"Your accent gave it away."

"My accent?"

"I'm just kidding." He laughed as he put his arm around

me tightly. Was this Southern friendly or regular flirting? "Libby told me when I delivered to her last night."

"Of course, I should have guessed." My landlord liked to gossip, didn't she?

"Since you're new here, I'd love to show you around. You should learn the places that are safe and the ones that aren't. Being such a pretty woman, I'd hate for you to see the wrong side of town."

"I need the vegetables now that the roux's finished," Frankie called out as she walked from the rear with a Bloody Mary in her hand. "Why, hello, Miss Sammy! Don't mind me and my drink."

Frank dropped his arm from around me and rushed behind the deli counter. "I'll take it back. Do you want me to put them in?"

"Yes, why don't you take over so I can rest for a minute?" she said while sitting down next to the cash register.

"Yes, ma'am," Frank answered. "Nice to see you again, Sammy. Hope I'll see you soon."

By Frank's quick exit, and Frankie's raised eyebrows toward her grandson, I knew his attention was flirting as opposed to Southern hospitality. I couldn't put my finger on it, but Frank was just a little too friendly. And the way he offered to show me around town was off-putting. I understood why he was single.

"Would you like a Bloody Mary while you shop? Don't tell anyone. I shouldn't offer alcohol, but I can't make gumbo without a drink to keep me company."

"Not today," I said. "What I really need is coffee. And something for lunch."

Although I insisted Frankie stay seated, she refused and was up and putting a can of Community Coffee, a small bag of sugar, a pint of half & half, and a roast beef po' boy sand-wich in my shopping basket.

"I almost forgot these," she said while grabbing Zapp's Voodoo Chips. "How about a sweet tea to go with it?"

"You know just what I need."

"I know what all my customers need," she said as she packed my groceries and handed me my drink. "Do you want Frank to deliver this for you? He'll finish in a minute."

"No, I'm good, but thanks." I couldn't help but smile to myself at Frankie's matchmaking attempt.

I arrived home and put my lunch on a table in the court-yard. The continued sunny weather was too perfect to pass up. After putting away my groceries, I grabbed Andrew's gift to read while I ate.

The crisp French bread held the sandwich perfectly. I knew to get it "dressed" which meant the roast beef was topped with shredded lettuce, tomatoes, pickles, and mayonnaise. Paired with my sweet tea and chips, it was another excellent meal, not that I was surprised.

Andrew's book was a surprise, though. From the title, *Voodoo: A Historical Perspective*, I expected it to be dry and academic. It was in a few sections, but he also shared great anecdotes from the religion's practitioners. Before I realized it, I finished the first twelve chapters.

As I flipped the page to the thirteenth chapter, I found Andrew's business card which included his cell phone number handwritten on it. I texted him, *Thanks again for an amazing book. your neighbor Samantha,* and almost dropped my phone when it immediately rang in my hands.

"Um, hello?"

"It's Andrew. I don't text."

"I'm so sorry! I didn't mean to interrupt your day."

"No, my dear, you didn't. I appreciate the message, but I prefer calling to texting."

"Good to know," I said, relieved I hadn't offended him. "I just had to tell you I love your book. It's informative, but also fascinating storytelling."

"Why thank you." I heard the pride in his voice. "That's a wonderful description. And that was my goal, so I'm honored you like my work."

"Are you writing anything now?"

"I am working on a book about Marie Laveau, the Voodoo queen as she's referred to in popular culture."

"Great. I'll want a copy."

"You're first on the list. I must go now, but thank you again for your kind words."

After we hung up, I went to the back of the book to see Andrew's author biography. It didn't say much except that he "is a lifelong history lover, a professor at NYU, but lives part-time in New Orleans." His picture was surprising in that it was a portrait of lightness I hadn't seen in him. The photograph was at least fifteen years old, but it wasn't age that made it different. A happier and less-serious man stared at me. Had the credited photographer, Samuel Baker, brought out the best in him?

There was no mention of his shop, so I checked the copyright on the book. He published it in 2004, the year before Hurricane Katrina. Was 2005 the year that changed Andrew? From what I understood about hurricanes, they appeared not only to change the landscape but also the people who survive them. Andrew and I might have that in common. Perhaps one day we would both be ready to share that information with each other.

11

I spent the rest of the day reading Andrew's book and posting on Instagram and Facebook. I enjoyed seeing my friends' reactions to my pictures. They were all positive, so perhaps they understood my move to New Orleans was permanent. It made for a nice relaxing evening after the previous nights out. I was more of a homebody in San Francisco, and I felt the need for a break from socializing.

I kept to my solitary routine the next morning as I drank coffee and settled down on my love seat with a notepad and pen in hand. I wrote out a to-do list which included researching platforms for my blog and running routes around the neighborhood. As I scribbled "do laundry," I looked at one of my suitcases waiting in the corner. It was full of wrinkled clean clothes and some dirty items. My move came so quickly that I threw things in my suitcase with no rhyme or reason. Time to try out the washer and dryer in the laundry room.

My overflowing basket blocked my view as I walked through the courtyard. I didn't need my vision to know I wasn't alone. I sensed eyes watching me. And there was that voice.

"Samantha, the machines are not available now."

I turned around and put my basket down to face Ruby. She took one step out of her doorway holding one of her cats.

"Good morning, Miss Ruby. I assume you're doing laundry."

"No, but I will be in forty-five minutes."

"I didn't know there was a schedule. Is it posted in the room?"

She stared at me as if I spoke another language. After an awkward pause, she said, "No, there isn't an official timetable. Seeing you have no obligations, I'm sure you can wait."

Now it was my turn to stare. "That's presumptuous. You know nothing about me."

"I beg to differ. I've read your cards and spoken to the spirits about you. I don't know everything about you, but I know enough."

"What is that supposed to mean?" I stepped closer to her and unlike before, she didn't flinch when I moved near her.

"You can shake your head at me, but I am being honest. You're lost, but you don't realize it. I'm not sure yet if you will find your way."

I just wanted to do my laundry and instead I was getting lectured by my crazy neighbor. As I tried to pick the words to say, a group of dolls sitting on a chair inside Ruby's apartment distracted me. While their hair colors and clothing varied, they were all the same type: BB dolls.

Ruby turned to follow my gaze, and when she spun back to face me, she was a different person. Gone was the smug spiritualist, and in her place was a frowning yet sad-eyed old woman clutching her cat.

"I've said what I needed to say," she whispered as she shut her door. I heard her mumbling, but I couldn't make it out. I stayed for a moment contemplating trying to get her to talk when a man called out.

"I would leave her alone. You don't want her to curse your laundry. I have firsthand experience."

"Seriously?" I said as I spun to face Connor. "I'm afraid to ask."

He picked up my basket and walked toward me. "I'll tell you the legend of my pink clothes over a cup of coffee. I even brought scones."

"A cursed laundry story and pastries? I can't resist." I grinned as I opened my door. "Come on in."

I brewed a fresh pot of coffee as Connor grabbed plates from the cupboard for the food. We sat at the kitchen counter, and then I insisted on hearing his tale.

"I mean, I can't prove it was Ruby, but I ignored her request to not do laundry. Why should I wait an hour for her to do it? I'd finish before she needed it, but apparently that was the wrong thing to do," he said in between bites of a blueberry scone. "So I go to take my clothes out of the machine and everything is pink. And no, I didn't leave anything red in there."

"What did you do?"

"I took it to my momma to find out what to do," he said. "Yes, I'm a momma's boy. As I passed Ruby's door, she stood there with a smirk on her face. And those cats smirked, too."

I couldn't stop laughing for a full minute and Connor joined in. "Come on," I said as I calmed down. "Something must have been in there. She's a tarot card reader, not a witch or anything, is she? I specifically requested the no-magical-neighbor apartment building."

"Then you're in the wrong town," he said when his laughter died down, too. "Really, Miss Ruby is harmless. She's just peculiar, and it's obvious there's some pain underneath that tough-old-lady armor."

Thinking about her reaction to the dolls I saw, I had to agree with Connor. It didn't make me like her, though. "I guess you're right, but she still is annoying, especially with the psychoanalyzing she keeps doing."

"Is it that she's doing it, or that she's right?" he asked as he took our empty plates and cups to the sink and washed them.

"I think she's wrong," I said as I grabbed a dish towel to dry off the dishes. "First, I'm trouble, and now I'm lost."

"Sammy, so many people come to New Orleans because they're lost. Some stay and some go. I hope you'll stick around."

"I plan on it," I said as I put away the last dried mug. "Since I can't do laundry, can you help me from getting lost?"

"So you believe Ruby?"

"No, I'm confused about all the other neighborhoods."

From my backpack I pulled out a map and my notebook, and for the next hour Connor made notes for me. He explained all the specific areas around the Quarter that included the Treme, Marigny, and the Bywater. He circled the streetcar stop closest to us that would take me to the Garden District. Now I had a personalized map which covered restaurants, museums, and bars.

It was an afternoon of New Orleans history, but also an easy discussion back and forth about each other. He found out that I had an English degree while his was in music. Our recent jobs were both the result of temporary work straight out of college. Neither of us knew what we needed to do next, but we both agreed we weren't where we wanted to be career-wise.

"Maybe Ruby meant we're both lost," Connor said as he folded my map and handed it to me. "I think I'm ready for a change. I admire that you came out here without a job."

"I suppose I am a bit lost," I said as I walked him to my door. "I want to get back to writing or something in that industry. Will you return to music?"

"I hope so. I guess I just needed some inspiration." He kissed my cheek before stepping outside. "Bye, now."

I shut the door before he could see my grinning face. I felt like a lovesick schoolgirl. Is this how the unknown diary writer began her romance?

12

———

Connor knocked on my door as he opened it. "Sorry, I forgot to tell you. We're having a party this evening in your honor. You are available, right?"

"Of course. When?"

"Hopefully we'll be rolling by eight, but you'll learn that everyone has their own sense of time here."

"That much I know about New Orleans."

"You're a quick learner." He kissed my cheek once again. Would he kiss me again tonight? On the lips...

A few hours later, Libby tapped on my door, waking me from a nap. "Sammy, would you help me get ready for the party?"

I joined her outside where it was clear she was in her element. Her joy was infectious as I helped her move around the wrought-iron furniture and set up a temporary bar in the back of the courtyard. I filled Libby in on my first days here. She smiled as I told her about meeting the neighbors and exploring the neighborhood. She only stopped smiling when I brought up Ruby.

"I should have warned you about her, darling. We all do our best to stay out of her way, but she's harmless," she said, but the last part didn't sound convincing.

"I plan to avoid her, especially after she claimed I was trouble," I said, and then I repeated Ruby's words about me.

"That's Ruby just being Ruby. I mean, it's not like you brought any trouble with you. With such few boxes and suitcases, you can't have much baggage. Ha, ha," Libby said as she busied herself with the chairs surrounding a table.

Since I was on a roll with awkward conversations, I continued with the information that Andrew claimed not to know about the diary either.

"Hmm, that is the strangest thing. Maybe he forgot about it, but he is so meticulous I can't imagine that happening. It's more likely I did."

"Okay, then I guess I'll keep the book and key until someone claims it."

"You do that. The key really makes a lovely necklace for you," she said while pointing at the key I was still wearing.

We finished the party preparations in companionable silence. From the mason jars filled with Gerber daisies to the unmatching yet coordinated plates, silverware, and glassware, Libby had a knack for making the area inviting and warm. I hoped to learn from her; if it wasn't a matching collection from a home store, I couldn't set a table to save my life.

"Well, it's about time! I was worried Sammy and I would have to roam the Quarter looking for food." Libby pretended to pout, but she was beaming at her son walking into the courtyard.

"Hi, sorry I'm late. Had a few things to do, but I'm here to do your bidding," Connor said as he hugged her. "Sammy, thanks for helping my momma. Doesn't she make every-thing pretty as a picture?"

"I agree," I said. "She's quite the artist and hostess."

"Oh, now hush, you two," Libby said as she smoothed down another tablecloth.

"It's party time!" yelled Neal as he skateboarded in with Matt and Joey following on foot.

"No, it's time to get the food at my restaurant," Connor announced. "Can you guys help?"

"Sammy, we're done here, so go with those boys to make sure they come back promptly," Libby insisted as she shooed us toward the gate. "Don't forget anything!"

I turned to see William joining his wife in the courtyard. With their arms around each other, they reminded me of parents watching their child and his friends head off to the first day of school. I couldn't help but smile back at them in return.

13

My short legs struggled to keep up with the long-limbed guys as I stopped for every corner musician or band. I couldn't help myself. Jazz drew me in like no other music. From the blare of a trombone to the sass of a clarinet, each note touched my heart and soul. Add a passionate voice to the mix and I was transported to another world. The joyful sounds filled the air, and people of all ages danced in the streets. Even those just standing or holding their cell phones to record the action appeared immersed in the experience.

"You're still a tourist, aren't you?" Joey laughed as Connor gently dragged me away from the third band.

"You'll go broke if you throw money to all of them," Matt said as he put a dollar in the band's tip jar.

"You can never get enough music. Am I right, gentlemen?"

"I agree with you," said Frank who walked up to us. Two large delivery bags weighed him down. "I always wished I played an instrument. How about you, Sammy? Are you a musician?"

"No, I just love music."

"But how do you feel about musicians?" Connor asked.

Everyone laughed but Frank. I sensed there was no love lost between them.

"Heading our way?" Neal said.

Our group strolled down Royal Street together. Connor, Matt, and Neal peppered Frank with questions about the number of tourists in town this year for Mardi Gras. The legend in the Quarter was the number of muffulettas Frankie's store sold in the upcoming weeks indicated the level of business the tour guides and restaurants could expect. They hoped for a busy season. Frank agreed to let Joey interview him for an urban legends paper he was writing for school.

I listened in on the conversation, enjoying the banter of the guys and all the new information I was learning about life in the area. Watching them walk ahead of me, I smiled as they reminded me of a boy band with their similar hair color and height. If they sang and performed a choreographed dance, they would earn a ton of money and the adoration of many young girls. And yes, older women like me, too.

I paused once more for a saxophonist playing a toe-tapping number. I enjoyed it until I saw the guys were half a block ahead of me. As I tipped my last dollar, a woman yelled behind me.

"Hey, Sam! Where have you been?"

In the past, I wouldn't have stopped for the name Sam, but it was close enough to my new nickname that I turned around. Her blonde ponytail bobbed up and down as she stomped in our direction. It impressed me that she moved that fast in her tight jeans and snug top. Her shiny red high heels didn't slow her down either.

As I stood there waiting for her to catch up, I realized she wasn't looking at me. I followed her gaze to see that she was marching straight toward my group of friends. Why did she yell "Sam" if she was talking to Matt, Neal, Joey, Connor, or Frank? They seemed confused, too, by the looks they gave each other. I wasn't close enough to hear their words, but with their shrugging shoulders and shaking heads, no one seemed to recognize the angry young woman.

"Hey! Wait up! Why haven't I seen you?" she called out, picking up her pace.

Were the guys walking faster, too? The woman must have thought the same thing after she came to a sudden stop by me. I watched as Frank bolted left onto Conti Street while I lost the others in the increasing crowds on Royal Street. Between the chatter of the pedestrians and a ten-piece brass band starting a new song, her one last cry of "Hey, come here" fell on deaf ears.

She stood there with anger radiating out of her entire body. Before I could talk to her, she breathed in deeply and exhaled loudly. With her head hanging, and her hands shoved in her jean pockets, she trudged back down the street. The word "ghosted" came to mind. From her words and actions, someone was ignoring her. It had happened to me a few times; it was always a guy I was dating who would disappear by not returning calls or texts. I recognized the signs, so I couldn't help but sympathize with her. Which one of my friends was ghosting her?

I knew our destination; otherwise, I would have been even more annoyed at the guys leaving me behind. I walked to the restaurant service door as Joey came out first. "Where have you been? Sneaking off to give money to another band?" he said as he carried out two foil-covered trays.

"Trying to get out of helping?" Neal joked while hoisting bags of ice on his shoulders.

"No," I snapped. "Didn't you hear the pretty blonde woman yelling? I swear she knew one of you or Frank."

They shook their heads no. I didn't believe them.

"Well, she was mad at someone," I said as I grabbed a sack of rolls from Connor's hands. "I guess I'm wrong."

"It wasn't me. I haven't pissed off any women since you," Connor said and winked at me. He closed the alley gate after Matt came through with a tray of chocolate chip cookies.

"I don't know who she is, I promise," Matt whispered. I half smiled back as he spoke again: "But she looks familiar..."

The blast of a trumpet player interrupted our conversation. I let the music distract me from the run-in with the stranger. I needed to forget that one of my friends must be lying... and why?

14

―――――

Once we got back to the building, the continuing preparations and Libby's contagious enthusiasm made me forget the incident.

"Time for you to relax, Sammy, and enjoy the evening!" Libby exclaimed as she positioned me as the guest of honor and returned to organizing everything and everyone.

Once Sissy arrived we started the party. Andrew was to join us later, William shared, although he said you never knew with Andrew. "Between his store and his interest in Voodoo, he's always busy."

"He gave me his book on Voodoo when I visited his shop. I assume he's not sacrificing chickens in the courtyard at midnight."

William nearly spit out his drink. "Sorry! I just got that visual in my head," he said as he checked his red polo shirt for stains. "He keeps to himself, but I don't think that's the Voodoo."

We walked over to the makeshift bar by the three-tiered fountain in the rear. Ferns filled it instead of water which softened the brick wall behind it.

"Why does he keep to himself?" I asked as William made me a Pimm's cup. "He seems confident, although a bit distant, but I can't explain why I feel that way."

As we walked back to the table, he said, "From what I gathered, Katrina turned his world upside down. Andrew lost his home and, I believe, some of his family. That's all he shared when he rented his apartment. Even Libby couldn't get more out of him. He's just one of the many people in this city who had to reinvent themselves after the hurricane."

Perhaps it was the second drink or the thoughts of hurricanes, but I drifted off. Suddenly I noticed everyone was looking at me.

"Sammy! Where did you go? You were a million miles away," Sissy asked as she walked over to me. "You're not dreaming of that diary, are you?"

"What diary?" Joey said as the group crowded around me.

"She found a journal in her apartment, but I didn't put it there. Or at least I don't recall," Libby said. "Can you get it? Maybe someone will recognize it."

"I didn't recognize it." Andrew walked in the courtyard. "The key is the interesting part of this mystery in my humble opinion."

I didn't believe Andrew ever had a humble opinion. From the looks of the group, I wasn't the only one who thought that. Matt raised his eyebrows at me, and Neal said something amusing under his breath based on Connor's stifled laughter.

"Oh, I am so glad you joined us!" Libby rushed over to Andrew who bent down to kiss her cheek. "I miss seeing you! You must be so busy with the shop."

His face softened at the sight of Libby. "I had to be here

to formally welcome our latest resident. Hopefully she'll be here longer than the last person."

"Poor Mark," Sissy said. "He was a lost soul. Could the diary be his?"

"No, he left the apartment empty," Libby said.

"Let's see this infamous diary," Matt said.

I got the journal and Matt reached for it first. He read a page and said, "No, I don't think it's Mark's."

He gave the book to Neal. Joey, Neal, and Connor thumbed through it together. Connor laughed, "You guys need to use this. It could be the love and romance tour."

William read it last and handed it to me. "I take it no one is claiming ownership of this?"

It was a resounding "no" from the group.

"Well, Sammy, this diary and key are definitely yours now," Libby called after me as I put the book away.

"Thanks, I guess," I said as I came back out, this time holding the mysterious gift bag. "How about this? I found it in front of my door the other day."

I took the doll out and held her up in the air.

"It's a BB doll!" Sissy grinned as she grabbed it out of my hand. "Every girl in New Orleans has at least one. Mrs. Betty Boudreaux made them and sold them in the French Market until she passed away."

Neal came over and looked over Sissy's shoulder. "I remember her. She was the sweetest lady. I bought a few for my nieces. No offense, Sammy, but you're a little old for dolls."

Everybody laughed, including me, but I wasn't laughing on the inside.

"I agree, but someone hoped I would like it. Come on, 'fess up," I said. Everyone shook their heads. "Well, whoever left this at my door didn't sign the card."

I took the doll back from Sissy. "Funny thing is, I already have one. It's the only toy I have from my early childhood." This statement led me into explaining my background: a shorter version, though, like I did the other night at Napoleon House. I left out the part about the photo I found in my mother's belongings, as I wasn't ready to share that information just yet.

The group surprised me as my orphan past didn't shock them. Libby's reaction bordered on pity, with her eyes tearing up as she pulled me into a hug. She changed gears as she released me and declared, "That's quite a story, but look at you now!"

"You must be a Southerner. No wonder you moved here." Matt smiled, as did the rest of the group. I heard "wow" and "can't imagine," but the kind faces of my new friends assured me they didn't feel sorry for me.

"Are you here to find your family?" Neal and Joey said in unison.

"Yes, I am curious about my past. I plan to start looking for my birth family soon," I said.

"Let us know if we can help. We're used to doing research," Matt offered.

"Yes, we do it all the time for our tours. I bet you do, too, Joey, for school," Neal added.

"That's my job," Joey agreed. "Sounds like you have a team to help you, if you want one."

"Thanks," I said. As happy as I was for the offers, I wasn't sure when I would be ready to share the photo with my new friends. Until I knew why my parents hid the picture, I would keep this information to myself for a bit.

"Well, my dear, you're full of mysteries with your history, the diary, and the doll," Andrew whispered in my ear as he kissed me on the cheek. "That key must be important, too."

And with that he nodded to the group and headed to his apartment.

"He always drinks and runs," Connor muttered as we watched Andrew leave.

"Oh, hush," Libby said as she picked up Andrew's empty glass of wine. "He rarely joins us, so he must think Sammy is as special as we do."

I blushed, and my friends raised their glasses in a toast. "To Sammy!"

The night continued with Neal and Matt setting their speakers on their balcony. Sissy tried to follow a new dance Joey said was the rage at the bars on Bourbon Street, but she swore he made it up because she couldn't get it. We all ended up just dancing as a group except for Libby and William who swayed on their own in the courtyard's corner.

The music and our laughter echoed off the brick walls as DJ Neal played an eclectic selection of music. From pop to rock to a few New Orleans tunes thrown in at my request, we danced for an hour. Connor had just taken my hand to dance to a John Coltrane number, when the sound of a bell interrupted the song.

We turned our heads to find Ruby standing in her doorway in a shiny orange kaftan ringing a handbell. She looked like a New Age schoolmarm. Joey slid over and whispered in my ear, "Are we in trouble?"

There was no way she heard him, but the look she gave us said otherwise.

"Oh my goodness, Ruby, I am so sorry!" Libby said as Neal turned off the music from his phone. "I knocked on your door to invite you, but I assumed you weren't home when you didn't answer."

William presented her with a glass of wine which I suspected was a peace offering.

"Thank you. You always remember I like red wine," Ruby said. "Libby, I've been communing with the spirits for hours, so I missed your invitation."

"Well, you're here now! We're welcoming our latest addition to the family, Sammy." Libby's smile faltered as she must have remembered my story about our meeting. "Oh, you've met."

"Yes." Ruby's voice didn't hide her annoyance, not that she was trying. "Joseph, do you live here now?"

"No, ma'am. Just here for the party."

"Thank goodness."

Could this woman be any ruder? Her behavior surprised me, but by the looks of the others, it was the norm for Ruby.

Ever-polite Sissy tried to defuse the situation. "Our dance party is ending, but would you like to join us for a drink? It's a chance to get to know Sammy. And you, too, Miss Ruby."

"You are always trying to make me talk, aren't you?" Ruby replied. "Now is not the time, so I will leave you to your nightcap albeit a quiet one, I hope."

With that she walked back to her door with her bell and the glass of wine. As she turned, I hoped that my unflinching stare would show her I wouldn't take her unkindness. Her hostile glare was not unexpected, but I saw her face reflect concern for a moment. Was it for me or for herself?

Her cats strolled out from the back of the courtyard and wrapped themselves around her legs before they all entered her apartment. Now, that was quite the way to exit a party, I had to admit.

15

The bang of her door signaled the end of our encounter with Ruby and the start of another round of drinks for everyone.

As Libby corralled us over to the back tables, farthest away from Ruby's apartment, she apologized to Joey and me about Ruby's behavior.

"I've met some strange people in my life, but she takes the cake," Joey said as he assured Libby he was not offended.

"Honestly, I can't get anything out of that woman, no matter how hard I try," Sissy complained.

"She must have a secret past," Neal said. "Or she's a serial killer. Or a Voodoo priestess with Andrew as her second-in-command."

"Oh now, stop that!" Libby reprimanded him, but giggled as she did.

"Another mystery for you, Sammy," Connor said as he smiled at me. "Are you going to play detective and discover the real reason for Ruby's secretive ways and Andrew's mysterious manner?"

"We should leave them alone. Everyone's got a past they'd like to forget, don't you think, son?" William said pointedly to Connor.

The silence that followed felt louder than the music from our dance party. Matt, Neal, and Sissy focused on their drinks while Joey and I looked at each other in confusion. Connor stood up, but sat quickly back down and took out his trumpet mouthpiece. As he fiddled with it, eyes downcast, Libby glared at her husband with her lips pursed. William shook his head, but I couldn't decide if it was out of frustration or surprise that his comment made that much of an impact.

The night was getting stranger by the minute. It was my turn to change the mood.

"I think I have enough mysteries for now." I laughed, hoping it sounded authentic. "In the meantime, let's figure out how we can put all this stuff away without Ruby ringing the bell at us again."

It was the right thing to say as everyone jumped up to help. Libby directed the group as she did during the setup, and the cleanup went quicker than I expected. William took a handful of empty beer bottles from my hands and placed them in a recycling container he pushed over. I followed his gaze over at Connor and Libby whispering to each other as they flung the cloths off each table.

William looked at them and sighed. "Sorry about what I said earlier, Sammy. I should leave well enough alone with my son. He's getting himself together and I should be happy about it."

I wasn't sure what to say, but I didn't have to as William continued. "Just be careful. Don't get too close yet, dear." He gave me a quick peck on the cheek. "I love him, I do, but I hate when he hurts people."

Before I responded, he rolled the recycling bin to the back of the courtyard. So many questions popped into my brain, but I distracted myself by helping Joey, Matt, and Neal put the tables away.

I thanked everyone for the wonderful party after we cleaned up. As expected, Connor tried to get everybody to join him for a late night stroll down Bourbon Street. No one wanted to go. I was tempted, but I hadn't forgotten William's advice.

Back in my apartment, I replayed the evening. It was a fantastic party, but the run-in with the screaming woman on the street still bothered me. Could I have been wrong about her yelling at one of my new friends? And the diary and the doll were still mysteries. Maybe someone would tell me the truth in private, but I wasn't counting on it.

16

My body ached when I woke up. The days of walking the Quarter and the nights of rich food and drinking had worn me out. I fumbled for my phone from the nightstand and caught up on the news and Facebook posts from the comfort and coziness of my bed.

I accepted friend requests from Matt and Neal and their invitation to like their Facebook business page. It looked generic, so I decided to offer them suggestions on how to spruce it up, next time I met them. I finally got up and made coffee. I curled up on my love seat and noticed the diary on my table. The unclaimed diary. I owned it now, so I might as well keep reading:

OCTOBER 9TH

Another magical day with my beloved. I have learned so much about New Orleans from him. I can see us settling down in the French Quarter after today's clue:

The French Quarter isn't just restaurants and bars. But let's start down that famous street known for its nightlife instead of the royal house it's named for. Bars will turn into homes as we come to the street named for a politician. You'll know our house when you see one with its green shutters protecting the door of a single yellow shotgun shack. It may appear to be falling down, but the foundation is as strong as our love can be. If you get to the road where the soldiers stayed, you've gone too far. We'll go inside to leave another mark of our true love.

I LAUGHED as I read the line "the foundation is as strong as our love can be." This guy worked hard for this girl's affection. If this was even a nonfiction book. Perhaps someone wrote it as a romance novel and placed initials around town as a marketing ploy. I would follow all the clues and hopefully find out if this was a guidebook or a real journal. If nothing else it had been a fun scavenger hunt so far. After I got showered and dressed, I headed out the door to the next stop of the mystery tour.

I popped into Libby's café for a scone and coffee to take on my outing. She wasn't there, so it made for a quick visit. Sweet potato scones were the day's special, and I had to try it. Biting into the warm, flaky pastry, with its creamy topping, reminded me of the sweet potato pie my mom would make on rare occasions.

It was the only Southern dish she cooked. "It's the only thing I can do," she confessed when I begged her to share other recipes from her childhood in Baton Rouge. My father would nod his head in agreement, and I would relent until the next time she baked it.

I took a sip of my coffee to offset the sweetness of the pastry and the melancholia that invaded my mind. My family wasn't affectionate or sentimental, but we had moments of fun and happiness. And I knew they loved me even if they rarely said it.

From the café, I strolled up to Bourbon Street. I passed by Connor's restaurant and was disappointed not to see him. I didn't expect him to be at work this early. He was probably nursing a hangover at a friend's house. A female friend perhaps. Ugh. I wouldn't moon over him. The diary had enough of that silliness.

I walked past the businesses, surprised that they were open and serving customers. Did they close at all? I didn't want to patronize them in the morning. Or anytime. The throbbing techno music, sticky floors from spilled cheap drinks, and the chaos of hyped-up tourists didn't interest me. Not that I didn't like bars, but I came to New Orleans for jazz, better cocktails, and the opportunity to chat with people without yelling.

Just as the diary said, the blocks became residential the farther I walked. From multistory town houses to shotgun cottages, I admired them all. Some were in excellent shape, while some needed a fresh coat of paint or a stairway railing fixed. Before long, I discovered I was at the corner of Bourbon and Governor Nicholls. The street named after a politician. I dashed halfway down the road to read the Barracks Street sign. This was the location from the diary.

I wandered up the avenue and studied each house. No one appeared to be home, but because many houses kept their shutters closed, it was hard to tell. In the middle of the block, I came upon a yellow, single shotgun cottage. With its peeling paint, dirty white trim, and faded green shutters, this had to be the place from the diary.

I double-checked the book; I found the house. The hairline cracks along the foundation confirmed it. I climbed the three chipped cement steps to read the paper tacked on the shuttered front door. A note from the construction company stated the work would continue next week. I was glad it was under repair; even in its disheveled state I saw the bones of a sturdy and charming home.

Now what? No initials on the shutters, so I opened them to check the door. I searched it from top to bottom, but found nothing. As I checked the left side, I glanced over at the unshuttered front window. Through one pane, writing was visible on a wall. I jumped down from the stairs and peered through the window.

I tried wiping it to get a better view, but dirt clouded the inside of the window. It looked like letters, but they were too far away for me to read them. I needed to know if the initials were there.

I stepped back up to the front door and noticed the unusual keyhole. Could this be the lock to the diary key? I took my necklace off when a voice interrupted me.

I was busted.

"Excuse me, miss. Can I ask you a question?"

"Sure," I answered, expecting a police officer to confront me, but found a middle-aged couple covered in beads and each holding an infamous grenade-shaped cup from a Bourbon Street bar.

"We're trying to find Marie Laveau's house. Do you know where it is?"

"Are you looking for her home or the Voodoo shop?"

"Her house," the woman said as she showed me a barrette, candy, and a piece of chalk in her hands. "I want to give her something so I can ask for guidance." The man with her rolled his eyes behind her back, but smiled at her as she twisted her head to glare at him. He might be the one in need of Marie Laveau's help if he did that again.

"The site of her old house is on St. Anne, but people leave offerings at her tomb in St. Louis Cemetery No. 1," I said as I took the map out of her companion's hand and pointed to the cemetery and the residence. "I recommend going on a New Orleans Past & Present tour and then stopping by Lagniappe Books for more info on the Voodoo queen."

They nodded their heads as I talked, but with their beverage choice at 10:30 a.m., I doubt if they really heard me. At least I'd shared the bit of history I had learned so far from Andrew's book and promoted Neal and Matt's business.

"Thank you," the woman said as she pulled her companion along who slurped the last of his drink. "We love your house!"

With a key in my hand, they assumed I was the home-owner instead of a burglar. It's not breaking and entering if I use a key. Not that it worked. That would have been too easy.

To the right of the home was the entrance to the alley that led to the backyard. Another lock to try, but as I went to put the key in the lock, the gate swung open. Whether it was luck or a contractor's incompetence, I took advantage of this opportunity. I checked the sidewalks in both directions; the area was empty. I entered and shut the door behind me.

I dodged building supplies and weeds as I followed the uneven pathway to the backyard. The fence surrounding the small courtyard must have been new, as it was free from invasive vines or scratches along its walls. A porta-potty sat in the far corner. I spotted no initials anywhere in the area.

With my key still in my hand, I headed to the back door. The lock looked similar to the one on the front door, so I knew it wouldn't work. As I put my necklace back on, I realized the door was ajar. I was already trespassing, but entering the actual house meant a bigger commitment to that act. Was the diary worth it?

Yes. I just had to know more about the journal. If I found the initials here, it would confirm the diary's authenticity.

But would it get me any closer to finding who wrote it and why they left it in my apartment? Maybe not, but I hoped for any answers at this point.

I came up with my excuses in case the police caught me. Sorry, Officer, I thought I heard a cat meowing in pain and I had to explore. Sorry, Officer, I'm a tourist and couldn't resist seeing a real New Orleans home. Hopefully, they would buy my lies.

It was too late to turn back as I stepped into the house and rushed to the front. I would be in and out before anyone realized I was here. Thick dust covered the living room. "Demo this wall next," "Don't touch the bricks," and "Use the porta-potty assholes!" decorated the wall, not romantic hearts with initials.

I checked the other walls, window trims, baseboards, and the fireplace, but found nothing. Was I in the wrong home? I was already inside, so I might as well look through the rest. The shotgun cottage style meant it only had a few rooms so a search would be quick.

According to the books I'd read, some homeowners renovate this type of house to include a hallway. Not this one. One room followed another, so I searched the bedroom next. Once again, no initials anywhere. Even the closet was empty except for a lone wire hanger and a mummified mouse.

I moved on to the kitchen where I opened and closed each cabinet after not finding any markings. Only a rusted cast-iron skillet remained. Coughing after slamming the last door shut, I caught my breath and stared at the only place left, the bathroom.

Based on the porta-potty note in the living room, I expected the bathroom to be a smelly, disgusting mess. The boyfriend had a horrible sense of humor if that's where they wrote their symbol of love. I twisted the doorknob, flung open the door, and braced myself for a sewer-like stench.

I couldn't say it smelled daisy fresh, but the room was just musty. A cracked porcelain sink was to the left of the door. On the opposite wall was a toilet which had seen better days. The showpiece of the bathroom stood in front of me, a freestanding claw-foot bathtub. It appeared to be original to the home, and its pristine condition surprised me. I assumed that's why someone had covered it in plastic.

I walked over to inspect the intricate details of the tub's feet. As I admired them, a flash of red caught my eye. I didn't notice red paint anywhere else in the house, but it looked like a dash on the edge of the tub. What a shame on such an otherwise beautiful piece. I moved forward to check it out.

No. No. No.

18

—————

I stumbled backward and fell against the dirty toilet. Fortunately, the lid was closed as I sat down to stare at the red high-heels poking out of the edge of the plastic roll in the tub. I recognized those shiny shoes..

Pushing myself up off the toilet, I tried to slow my breath before I made my way back to the bathtub. With shaking hands I peeled the outer layer of the plastic to see the contents of the tub. It might just be shoes tucked in a pile of construction trash. I gasped after the wrapping slid to the floor, exposing the body.

While my eyes registered the red high heels, tight jeans, and snug shirt, my brain wasn't making the connection. How could it be the woman from the street? Why would she be here?

I clutched the edge of the tub as my knees buckled underneath me. My face was within inches of last night's stranger. I peered into her cloudy pupils. Her smeared crimson lipstick emphasized the frozen yell of her mouth. She no longer was searching or screaming for a man in the crowd, for the man who ghosted her. She was now a ghost.

Or an angel as last night's ponytailed blonde hair fanned out around her head like a halo. Streaked with dried blood and dust, her face still appeared young and innocent, unmarred by wrinkles of a fully lived life.

Her angelic pose continued with her arms folded across her chest while clutching a BB doll. The sweet doll should have made me smile, but the small note card in her arm negated any charm. "RIP SARAH" wasn't the message I expected since the last time I found one of these dolls it said "Welcome Home." I didn't feel welcome anymore.

I pushed myself up from the tub and reached for the card, but pulled my hand back. It was part of a crime scene and I couldn't grab it. I had already touched too many places and items in this house. Stupid me, but I didn't expect to find a body. Damn that diary.

Now I knew there was more to the book than the romantic musings of a woman: this dead woman called Sarah. Why did the journal lead me here? And why was she killed? Was that the whole point of the book?

I flipped the plastic back over her out of respect and in the hope I would calm down if I didn't have to see her body. It might have worked if I hadn't dropped my phone behind the sink as I tried to leave the room. It fell next to a lead pipe propped up in the corner. With dried blood and wispy strands of blonde hair clinging to one end, it must have been the murder weapon.

I closed the bathroom door and stood in the middle of the kitchen. I wrapped my arms around myself in the hope I would stop shaking like a wet Chihuahua. Stomach acid inched up my throat, and I tasted the earlier pleasant mix of coffee and sweet potato. I gulped it back down and bit my lip to keep from vomiting.

I needed to leave there before I threw up, but I needed to

call for help. My phone showed "no service." I was in a cell phone dead zone. No, a real dead zone. Time to go before I lost my breakfast, along with my sanity.

I yanked open the door in the hope the fresh air and cell phone reception would calm me down. Instead, I ran into a man filling the doorway. I screamed and fell backward onto the hard kitchen floor, praying I wouldn't die next.

19

―――――

"Whoa, Sammy, what's going on?"

Shocked to hear my name, I opened my eyes. The blinding sunlight behind the figure caused me to squeeze them shut again.

"Hey, it's me. What's wrong?"

I forced my eyes open to find the kitchen wasn't as bright since someone closed the door. I looked up to a man I recognized, but instead of comfort I felt confused.

"F-Frank?" I stammered. "What are you doing here?"

"I was making a delivery in the neighborhood. I saw you come in here," he said as he stepped closer to me. "The gate was open, so I came in here. Since it's a construction site, I wanted to make sure you were okay."

Was he following me? He had to be lying about the gate. I knew I closed it. I scooted back toward the cabinet thinking about that frying pan again. Before I had to decide if I needed it, we were interrupted.

"Frank! What's going on? Who screamed?" demanded the elderly man wielding a baseball bat as he flung open the back door. "Are you a thief, young lady? A drug addict?"

"No," I said while I got up off the floor. "I was exploring and I found a body."

The bat fell and landed with a thud on Frank's feet. I had to give Frank credit; he didn't flinch or yell. He picked up the bat, all while making eye contact with me.

"I bet the neighborhood kids are playing a joke," he said. "I'm sure it's nothing."

He may have meant it kindly, but it was patronizing. "I know what I saw. It's a dead woman, and I recognized her from last night."

"What are you talking about, Sammy?" he said. He took his usual toothpick out of his mouth and shoved it in his front pocket. Instead of looking at me with his typical flirtatious intentions, I thought Frank was angry or confused with me. Or both.

"Frank, who is this drunk lady?" the man asked while he studied me through his thick glass lenses. I'm certain I looked intoxicated, or worse, covered with construction dust.

"I am not drunk," I said as I tucked loose hair behind my ears. "I'm looking for, well, I was on a scavenger hunt and ended up here."

I didn't want to explain the diary to the stranger. Was it a coincidence Frank saw me here, or did he know about the diary?

"I found a dead woman in the bathtub." I shoved my shaking hands in my pockets and stood up straight so I would appear normal and not inebriated or crazy.

"I bet it's just a joke. Don't worry." Frank's cheerful demeanor returned as he winked at me before he walked to the bathroom door. "Mr. Gregory will stay here with you while I check it out."

My new guardian snatched the bat and planted his

orthopedic shoes on the cracked linoleum floor. "I'll protect this young lady while you find out what's going on." His weapon wobbled in his weathered hands and I sighed. Mr. Gregory nodded at me; he must have thought I was happy to have him as a bodyguard. No, I just couldn't believe the situation I was in.

The bathroom door creaked as Frank opened the door. He sauntered into the room. My nausea returned when I recognized the crinkling sound of the plastic being unwrapped. I leaned over the rust-stained kitchen sink, trying once again to control my stomach and emotions.

"Are you okay? There's really a body in there, isn't there?" Mr. Gregory said. He placed the baseball bat on the chipped Formica counter. "The neighborhood is changing. I miss the days when neighbors were friends, and we looked out for each other."

His glasses distorted his watery brown eyes, reminding me of a forlorn basset hound. I wanted to comfort him, but there was nothing I could say that would make this situation any better for him or his neighbors or his world.

"I'll be all right," I said. "How did you end up here?"

"I live across the street and I noticed Frank looking in the window. Then he went down the alley, so I checked on him," he said while patting my white-knuckled hand on the edge of the sink. "The owners don't take kindly to people exploring, especially after someone broke in last month."

"Really? Did they steal anything?"

Mr. Gregory shook his head. "Funny thing is, they didn't take stuff or make a mess. The workers said just a few things looked out of place."

The construction company must not have been too concerned since I found the back door unlocked. Or did someone make it easy for me to get in?

"We need to go outside now," Frank commanded as he ushered us to the backyard.

"Damn, it's true, ain't it?"

He nodded his head as he dialed 9-1-1. He walked to the side of the house, I assumed to find a signal. Mr. Gregory and I stood together like strangers at a party, not knowing what to do or say. Finally, I spoke up.

"I'm sorry about all this."

"Nothing to be sorry about, unless you killed her," he said. "No, I know you didn't. You have a kind face, and if Frank trusts you, then I do, too. He's a good boy, from a good family."

I looked over at Frank on his phone. His calmness and efficiency were reassuring, but last night's run-in with the now dead woman bothered me more. Did he happen to see me going into the house, or was he following me? Was the woman in the bathtub a stranger to him? I should have gone with him in the bathroom to analyze his reaction.

I returned Mr. Gregory's smile with a thank-you. I wanted to ask him more questions, but Frank ended his phone call and joined us.

"The police are on the way," he said as he put his arm around me. I wanted to lean into him, but my distrust kept me from taking the comfort I needed. "I called my nonna and she'll call Libby for you."

Thankfully, I already had people who would be there for me in a crisis. Hopefully, there would be family and friends to mourn Sarah. Were one of my friends among them?

20

After verifying it was a dead body in the house, the police officers separated us. Mr. Gregory only went with a patient officer after I insisted I was fine. At least he was now on my side. The officer taking my statement didn't appear to feel the same.

"So, you're saying, you trespassed because you were following clues in a book?" the policeman said as he chewed on his pencil. "That's one helluva scavenger hunt."

I couldn't disagree with him. Appearing to be a silly romance, this diary now was turning into a horror story. I needed to read the next entry, but I didn't have any time between this skeptical officer questioning me and the detective that showed up next.

"Ms. Richardson, I'm Detective Armstrong." The man introduced himself with a firm handshake. "I need to take you up front to ask you a few questions. Is that okay?"

The badge hanging around his neck confirmed his police status; otherwise, I would have thought he was a bodybuilder dressed in his best suit. With his large muscles he was imposing, but his slow Southern drawl and kind eyes put me at ease. I bet he played good cop to his partner's bad cop.

We walked through the gate to a different scene than only an hour earlier. They cordoned the street off with police cars and yellow crime scene tape. Bystanders were standing in rows up to the tape, some with cell phones raised over their heads to take photos. Police officers, crime scene investigators, and other people whose jobs I couldn't figure out, roamed the blocked-off section. I tried to make myself small so I would go unnoticed by the photographers. I didn't want this to be my fifteen minutes of fame.

The detective insisted I sit on the front steps while he took notes as I talked. Fortunately, he wanted a quick version, but it didn't stop me from shaking again as I described finding the body.

"It's okay to be upset; you've had quite a shock," he said as he signaled a paramedic over. "Michael will check you out. I'll be right back."

The thermal blanket the EMT gave me helped a little, but I kept shaking, realizing I had more to tell the detective. How would I explain I recognized the woman from last night? More importantly, how would I tell him that the dead woman appeared to know one of my friends? Before I could figure out how not to implicate my friends, two familiar voices rang out above the noisy scene.

"Sammy! We're here!" Behind the crime scene tape stood my neighbors, my friends. Libby called to me while Sissy appeared to be arguing with the police officer keeping the crowds back.

"Rob! It took us twenty minutes to get here, so you better let us get to Sammy!" Sissy shouted as the detective walked through the alley gate toward me.

Detective Armstrong, Rob, I now assumed, stared at Sissy who crossed her arms, tapped her foot, and glared at him. He looked back at her and then at me. "Oh, I know who you are now," he said. "You're Sammy, Sissy's new friend. This isn't how I wanted to meet you."

I tried to smile, but I didn't have the energy. "Yes, I'm Sammy. Let me guess, you're Sissy's boyfriend."

"I was this morning. Hopefully, I'll still be if I get you to them quick enough." He grinned for a moment, then put on his serious detective face. "Frank and Mr. Gregory have confirmed your story, so I can let you leave. I know where you live, so my partner and I will come by later today."

"Thank you," I said as I took his offered hand to stand up. "I appreciate it."

We walked over to Sissy and Libby who both tried to lift the crime scene tape to let me through. Rob grabbed the tape and held it firmly in place.

"Now, ladies, I understand you're concerned about Miss Sammy, but I need to go over a few things," he said to my friends. Libby nodded, but Sissy raised her eyebrows at him and tapped her foot once again. Apparently, he was used to it as he continued talking.

"Take your friend home quickly as she's had quite the shock. The streets are already backed up, so it would be quicker for y'all to walk than have an officer drive you. Can you walk, Miss Sammy?"

"Yes, thank you."

"Good. Get some rest, and like I said, we'll be by later. In the meantime, please don't talk to anyone about this, especially the press. I can count on your discretion, can't I?" Rob directed his last comment to my friends.

Libby objected, but Sissy stepped in front of her and

addressed her boyfriend, "Of course you can. Just like we can count on you sharing any information, right?"

She gave him a quick peck on the cheek while lifting the crime scene tape and pulling me toward her. I fell into her arms, and the tension of the day spilled out of me.

"You're not going to pass out, are you?" Sissy asked as she pulled back from our embrace and looked me up and down. "Libby, call that EMT over."

"No, I'm fine, really." I smiled to convince them. "I'm exhausted and still can't believe this happened." I took off the thermal blanket and handed it to the paramedic who came over. "I just want to go home."

Libby squeezed my hand and pulled me through the group of people who were starting to take notice of me. "Let's get you home, darling."

The crowd stared at us, but then the coroner's van opened and a gurney was removed. Everyone was distracted, so we rushed away. We made it a few houses away when Frank yelled.

"Hey, Sammy! You, okay?"

"I'm fine. Are you two okay?"

"I'll be better when I get my bat back," Mr. Gregory griped as he steadied himself on Frank's arm. "Damn fool cops are calling it evidence even though I told them it's mine, and I brought it to the house."

"I'm sorry," I said, and I meant that about the bat and everything else that afternoon. His neighborhood would be a crime scene and tourist attraction for the rest of the day and night.

"It's New Orleans; crazy stuff happens," Frank said. "Can't say I've ever seen a dead body out on my deliveries, though."

"I'm sure it's not the first murder in the neighborhood,

but I hope it's the last," Mr. Gregory said as he and Frank walked past us.

Me, too, Mr. Gregory. But I also couldn't help but wonder if his arrival prevented me from becoming the second body in that house today?

21

———

I watched Frank guide Mr. Gregory to his home. A man and a woman of similar age were already waiting for him with looks of curiosity and concern. Although he told me how the neighborhood was changing, I felt better knowing he still had neighbors who cared for him.

And there was Frank. He had Mr. Gregory's key and was ushering him into his home, along with his friends. Was it really kindness or an act? I needed to talk to Frank about the woman, but it wouldn't be today.

We walked home via Royal Street instead of Bourbon Street. As locals, I was sure Libby and Sissy didn't want to stay on that road to battle the evening crowds wandering in and out of bars vying for patrons. The thought of the constant yelling, sticky sidewalks, and happy-go-lucky tourists brought back my nausea. I took a few deep breaths trying to calm myself. It helped, but what worked better was the warm embrace of my favorite grocery store owner.

"Oh, Sammy! What a terrible thing to happen to you," Frankie cried as she squeezed me like a boa constrictor. "I can't believe it." She finally pulled away from me and made the sign of the cross. "I will light a candle for her at the cathedral once Frank gets back."

Sissy and Libby also made the sign of the cross. Religion wasn't part of my childhood or adulthood, but I might need it after today. Frankie brought us inside the store and insisted on putting together dinner to bring home. Eating was the last thing on my mind, but she wouldn't take no for an answer.

"What's happening to the neighborhood?" Frankie sighed as she gathered enough food for a small army. "We used to have so many families living here. The kids would run up and down the streets, and the adults would sit and talk on the front steps."

"That's what everyone tells me," Libby said as she nodded to a bottle of whiskey Frankie held up before putting in the second grocery bag she started. "I wonder if that girl is from the neighborhood. So sad."

"Well, the owners can now sell the house and call it haunted," Sissy said as she shook her head to Frankie's offer of peppermint schnapps.

"Sissy!" they yelled at her in unison. I assumed she was joking, although I wondered about the "Haunted/Not Haunted" real estate signs around the Quarter.

"Oh, I'm just trying to add some levity to the situation," Sissy explained. "Frank would tell us if he knew the girl. Hopefully, someone just used the house as a dump site."

Before I could explain that I recognized the woman in the bathtub, the shop door flew open, and the two boys from my first visit bounded inside.

"Hey, Miss Frankie, did you hear about the body?" the older boy asked.

"They said Frank found her," the younger brother said

as he picked up a candy bar. "Do you think Marie Laveau killed her?"

"Hush, you don't know what you're saying," Frankie scolded them while looking at me and giving me the *boys will be boys* look.

"But, Miss Frankie, there was blood everywhere and Voodoo dolls," the young boy squealed. "Ouch, don't hit me!" His brother had slapped him upside his head and then took the candy bar from him.

"I'm sorry, Miss Frankie, my brother is just repeating what he heard," the older boy said.

"I understand, darling, but you shouldn't say bad things like that," Frankie admonished the boys in a firm but kind voice.

"Frankie! Is your grandson okay?" asked a flushed-faced woman who burst into the store. "My neighbor claimed Frank stopped a man from killing a girl down on Bourbon Street!"

"No, he found a bloody body!" the little boy interjected.

This was too much for me and I strode to the door. Libby and Sissy grabbed our bags and quickly followed me. I said thank you to Frankie. I doubt she heard me as the three customers were bombarding her with questions.

Outlandish stories were flying around the Quarter already, and I hoped my name wasn't associated with them yet. I wanted to return to my apartment with no other distractions. I was out of luck as Neal, Matt, and Joey were sitting in the courtyard drinking beers.

"Matt, you've got to stop booking senior citizen groups. I swear I can't walk that slow." Neal laughed as he opened up a bottle and handed it to Joey. "The tour took at least an extra thirty minutes, and instead of tipping they pinched my cheek and told me to wear a vampire cape next time."

Joey howled while Matt shook his head. "Neal, they didn't pinch your cheek, and it only took fifteen extra minutes. We can't always have bachelorette parties."

"I told y'all you need a gimmick. Looks fade, dude," Joey said. "Hey, ladies! Join us for a beer. The guys are telling me all about today's tours."

Matt stood up and walked over. "What's wrong, Sammy? You're as pale as a ghost."

"Did you take a competitor's ghost tour?" Neal joked.

Joey came over and pulled out the chair by my front door. "Sit down, Sammy, and tell us what's going on. Miss Libby, what happened?"

Libby sat down in the chair next to me and held my hand. "Sissy, why don't you explain?"

Sissy gave the boys a brief explanation of my discovery. Channeling my inner Nancy Drew, I studied their reactions. All three appeared surprised, nothing more.

Matt kneeled in front of me and stared at me, and said with such sincerity, "Sammy, I'm sorry. What a shock." He stood halfway up and gave me a hug. "We're here for you."

"Wow, that's crazy." Joey stepped into Matt's place and gave me a quick embrace. "That sounds awful, but I'm glad you're okay."

Neal moved Joey aside to hug me next. "All your friends are here for you. But wow, a body? Who was it?" Neal tried to question me, but the rapid footsteps filling the courtyard distracted all of us.

"Libby! I went to the café, but they said you ran off and yelled something about murder. Who's dead?" William demanded and Libby rushed over to him in the entryway.

"I'm fine. It's poor Sammy. No, she's not dead." Libby hugged him while explaining and you could see him relax into her embrace. "She found a dead girl in an empty cottage on Bourbon."

"Thank God! Sammy, are you all right?"

I nodded and stood up with what felt like noodle legs. "I'd like to go inside."

"Good idea. Let's take this food to your kitchen." Sissy picked up the bags and took my key and unlocked my door. Libby and William followed her in as I paused at the doorway.

"It'll be okay, Sammy."

"We're here for you."

"Call us if you need us."

Neal, Matt, and Joey all said those kind words before I shut the door behind them. Their remarks seemed sincere and their shock was reassuring. The reactions and shows of concern were what I expected from my friends, but I couldn't help but wonder if one of them was faking it. Like Frank, I still wasn't sure if any of them were lying about knowing the yelling woman from last night who was now the dead woman from today.

22

L ibby, Sissy, and William took charge as we settled into my apartment. Sissy wrapped a soft, knitted blanket around my shoulders before she began putting away the groceries from Frankie. Libby brewed coffee. "Good, you have the brand we like."

William brought over my mug with a "little liquid courage" as he called it when he poured a dash of whiskey into it. It was the best cup of coffee I'd had, but it wasn't just the alcohol calming me down. Watching my new friends take care of me gave me a sense of peace that I hadn't felt for a long time.

A knock broke my moment of Zen. I spilled my drink, but Libby and Sissy cleaned it up while William answered the door.

Detective Rob Armstrong, now known as Sissy's boyfriend, filled the doorway. "Hi, Mr. William. We need to talk to Miss Sammy."

"Come in," he said as he shook Rob's hand. "Hi, Christine. Nice to see you, but I'm sorry it's under these circumstances."

He returned the woman's handshake and ushered them in. With her perfectly tailored gray suit, cropped brown hair, and delicate gold earrings, she looked like a CEO, but the gun and badge on her waistband said otherwise.

"Same here," she replied. "Miss Richardson, I'm Detective Christine Gammon. We'll have you come to the station tomorrow for a formal statement, but we'd like you to answer a few questions now."

"I'm happy to help, but first, can you tell me the woman's name? Was it Sarah like the card said?"

Rob was moving both kitchen stools to the living room when he began to talk, but his partner interrupted him.

"We're still working on that," she answered as she sat down on a stool. Her long legs easily reached the floor. "We should have more information soon. I understand you were following a book that led you to the house. Is this correct?"

"Yes, I was following these clues I found in a diary. Sissy, can you hand me my backpack?"

She brought it over and stood behind me. I couldn't see her, but from Rob's face I gathered Sissy was giving him a significant glare. He rolled his eyes before returning to his serious detective expression.

"I shouldn't have trespassed, but I was curious..."

I handed the book to Detective Gammon, who began reading through it. Rob looked over her shoulder as she read each page. When she got to the entry about the house, she stopped and stared at me.

"Where did you get this?"

"I found it in the apartment." I pointed to the bookshelf. "No one knows where it came from."

"She's right. I didn't put it there. I bought a box of books from Andrew, but he didn't recognize it either," Libby said.

"That's Andrew who lives here, correct?" Rob asked as he opened his notebook and wrote more notes.

"Yes, but I'm sure he has nothing to do with this," Libby said as she drummed her fingers on the kitchen counter. William gently covered her hand to stop her and then held it.

"Me, too," Sissy said as she moved around the love seat to stand closer to Rob.

"We'll just check with him as procedure," Rob said. "There's nothing to worry about."

"We need to keep the book for now," Detective Gammon said. I watched in horror as Rob unfolded a plastic evidence bag from his jacket pocket. The diary slipped into the bag and out of my reach.

Mentioning the book to the police was necessary, but I should have finished reading it first. Racking my brain for a way to ask for it back, I was at a loss. Feelings of stupidity and anger overwhelmed me. I couldn't solve the mystery of the diary without it.

I tried to hide my emotions, but apparently it showed on my face. Detective Gammon's stare made me uncomfortable, and I understood how people confessed to crimes that they hadn't committed. After what seemed like minutes, but was only seconds, she asked, "You're sure you don't know who wrote this? Or is this something you did?"

Before I denied it, Libby did for me. "Of course she didn't do this! How could you say that?"

"I have to ask, Miss Libby. This isn't personal about Miss Richardson. But we have a dead woman whose family deserves the truth. You would want the same for your family, wouldn't you?"

The room was quiet. The reality of the situation came back into perspective. From the grim expressions to the momentary silence, I wasn't the only person thinking about Sarah and what her family and friends would face today.

"Forgive me. I'm just protective of my family," Libby said and then she sat down next to me and put her arm around me. I smiled back at her and relaxed into her.

"Sammy wasn't involved in this crime. I was with her when she found the first initials from the entry about Napoleon House," Sissy said while poking her finger on the front page of Rob's notebook. "Write that down in your book."

I caught Detective Gammon grinning for a moment; she must be used to Sissy's commands to Rob and enjoyed them. He ignored Sissy and spoke to me, "Let's hear about the initials."

I explained that I found the same initials, S + K, on the float display and at Napoleon House. Since the note on the doll was about Sarah, I assumed that was the S in the set.

"Was the doll hers? The BB doll?"

"Why do you ask?" Detective Gammon said.

"It was strange to see it because someone left one for me the other day. The card wasn't signed."

"That doll?" She pointed at my bookshelf.

"No, that's my childhood doll. The new one is in that gift bag on the kitchen counter, along with the note."

"Okay, can we take it? It may be related," Rob asked, but he already had another evidence bag. "Are you sure you don't know the victim?"

"I don't know her, but I saw her last night."

Libby gasped, and then the room fell silent again. Detective Gammon and Rob didn't express any emotion, but my friends looked shocked. I did just drop a bomb on them. I should have warned them on our walk home. I was making a mess of everything.

"You mean, Connor, Neal, Matt, and Joey were with you? Frank, too? Who was she calling for?" William asked before the detectives. He appeared as worried as he did earlier when he thought something had happened to Libby.

"Yes, Miss Sammy, who was she looking for?" Rob said while turning over a new page in his notebook.

"I'm sure it wasn't one of them. The streets are so crowded, and those boys look similar to each other and every other handsome man in the Quarter," Libby said as she got up from the couch and went to the kitchen. As she put the leftovers away, she asked, "Right, Sammy?"

I nodded at Libby and to the detectives. I didn't believe it, but I didn't want to upset Libby anymore today. "Is there anything else you need? I'm sorry, but I'm really exhausted."

Sissy came over and put her hand on my forehead and then took my pulse. "It would be best if Sammy got some rest now. Do you have enough information for tonight?"

The detectives looked at each other and then back at me. "Yes, but please come to the station tomorrow morning so we can take your fingerprints and ask a few more questions. You don't have plans to leave town, do you?" Detective Gammon said as she shook my hand and gave me her business card.

"No, I'll be there. Is nine okay?"

"That would be perfect. Thank you and get some rest," Rob said. "Sissy, I'll call you later."

They left, and the room seemed less tense, but it wasn't relaxed by any means. Libby tried to make small talk as she finished putting away the groceries and Sissy fluffed the pillows on my bed.

William checked the locks on my windows. "Will you be okay by yourself tonight? You can stay with us if you're scared," he said.

"You can come upstairs with me," Sissy called from my bedroom. I noticed Libby kept quiet.

"No, I'm fine. I'm so tired that I'm sure I'll fall asleep quickly." I put on a smile as I got up from the couch. "Everyone has been so kind today. I can't thank you enough."

Libby finally spoke, "We're here for you! You're one of us, remember?" She kissed me on the cheek and followed William to the door. "Call if you need anything." I heard their animated voices as they walked down the courtyard toward the front.

"Don't worry about Libby." Sissy was carrying an empty coffee mug from my bedroom. "She worries about Connor. And Frank, Matt, and Neal, and by extension, Joey. She is a momma bear." She washed the cup and the other dishes in the sink. "Do you really think the girl knew one of them?"

While I believed the woman knew at least one of them, I answered, "I don't know." But what I wanted to say was I hope not.

23

"It was good to meet your boyfriend," I said as Sissy handed me a plate. She wouldn't take no for an answer, so I accepted the meal. "I'm sorry it happened this way, though."

"Me, too. Rob's a great guy," Sissy said as she sat down next to me on the love seat with a plate of her own. "He and Christine have a near perfect clear rate, so they'll find out what went on with that poor girl."

"They seem like a good pair. Detective Gammon is a bit more serious than Rob, but I imagine that works for them."

She laughed before she said, "You figured that out quick. She puts up with him pretty well. I'll try to get more info out of him tonight. You'll learn more tomorrow morning, I'm sure."

I nodded as I took another bite of lasagna. The layers of pasta and ricotta cheese covered with an earthy tomato sauce warmed my stomach and soul. Frankie knew what her customers needed. And Sissy also knew what I needed as she poured us both a glass of wine.

After we finished our meal, my friend insisted on

washing dishes again, but this time she let me dry them. It felt good to do something as normal as eating dinner and cleaning up afterward. Tomorrow morning would be anything but ordinary, and although Sissy assured me it would be fine, my nerves hadn't gone away.

I locked the door behind Sissy and wandered over to the bookshelf where I found the diary. I inspected each book from the shelf to see if it was a duplicate or companion to the journal. Each one matched the title on its cover, so no surprises. Not that I expected to find an answer on the shelves; that would have been too easy.

If I still had the diary, I could read where the boyfriend took her to next. Unless the house was the last stop on their mysterious love tour. I always assumed the scavenger hunt ended with a romantic proposal somewhere iconic in the French Quarter. Was Sarah's murder the point of the book?

I poured another glass of wine to steady myself to check the internet. There were only bare-bone facts about the crime on news websites. Local neighborhood boards featured similar information, although some repeated the same lies the boys spouted in Frankie's store. I checked all the photos and didn't see me, except the back of my head in one grainy shot. Hopefully, no one would recognize me.

As I closed my laptop, a gentle knock at my front door made me jump. Who was out there at this late hour? The person knocked once more, so I decided not to ignore it. I assumed it was Sissy making sure I washed my wineglass. Or it could be the murderer.

I was just being ridiculous. Slowly, I opened the door as if that would stop a killer. I was acting more like a victim than a detective tonight. Instead of a knife, the handsome man wielded flowers. This time the mixed bouquet was wrapped in yellow tissue paper with a sticker from Frankie's store.

"Hey, I'm sorry. Here I am knocking at your door late at night again." Connor smiled, then his voice took on a serious tone. "Momma called me. This was the first chance I had to sneak away. Are you okay?"

"I'm fine," I said. I didn't want to cry on his shoulder. Yes, I did, but last night's doubt lingered. "The flowers are very sweet. Would you like to come in for a drink?"

"Now it's your turn to offer me a late night beer," he said with a smile. "I wish I could, but I have to go back to the restaurant. I just wanted to check on you."

"Thanks for thinking of me."

He hugged me and kissed my cheek. For a moment, I lost myself in his embrace. Sarah's dead body once again superseded my warm and fuzzy thoughts of Connor.

As he walked toward the street, I called out, "And thanks for the party last night. Did you keep it going on Bourbon? I thought maybe the guys joined you after all."

"You're welcome. No, I decided not to go out. I didn't want to dance alone," he said and waved as he raced out the gate.

He was charming all right, but was he also a liar? I fell into bed wondering if he was one, or if Frank, Neal, Matt, and Joey were liars, too.

24

————

Morning came quickly with the buzzing of my alarm and my phone. Sissy and Libby texted to check on me. I messaged back that I was fine, and I would text them after my police station visit. I bet Rob had orders to call his girlfriend the minute I left, though.

Libby also said I would find a bag of scones outside my door. I found them along with a copy of the local newspaper with the article about the body circled. A Post-it note on it said, *You're not mentioned by name, so don't worry. We're here for you. William.*

The scent of blueberry scones escaping the bag hit me as I opened my door. I made a pot of coffee, ate a scone, and read the brief newspaper article. While the press hadn't found me, they learned that Mr. Gregory was a witness. The reporter quoted him: "The nice young lady shouldn't have been trespassing, but it's worse that a murderer used our neighborhood for evil. Once I get my bat back from the police, I'll be on the lookout." I envisioned him out on his steps with his weapon in hand protecting his home and neighbors.

The newspaper report didn't include Frank's name. I thought he might have talked to the press, if nothing else for more exposure for the grocery store. Finding a body isn't the typical publicity a business looks for, though. Or could it be that Frank didn't want to be connected with the woman, Sarah? That wasn't fair; it was natural if Frank didn't want to to be associated with a murder. I know I didn't.

As I locked my front door to go to the police station, I looked down to find one of Ruby's cats brushing up against my legs. "Hi, pretty girl," I said as I bent over to scratch her on her head and to read the name Cleopatra on her name tag. She and I were becoming good pals. Her mother and I, not so much.

"Please don't distract her," demanded the voice of my least favorite neighbor. "I need to bring her back inside."

I braced myself, standing up to face Ruby, expecting another spiritual diagnosis from her. Instead, she stepped closer to me and spoke so softly I could barely hear her.

"I understand you discovered a body yesterday. Was it a teenager? A girl? Was she killed recently?"

"A woman in her twenties. She was murdered the other night," I answered. "Why do you ask?"

She sighed, from disappointment or relief, I couldn't tell. "Oh, just curiosity."

I wasn't a psychic, but I knew a lie when I heard one.

She picked up her cat and went to her front door. "I was right about you and trouble. Instead of following it, you find it."

That was the Ruby I knew. I gave her my best fake smile and headed to the courtyard gate. To my surprise, she murmured to her cat, "Yes, we'll keep looking out for her, Cleopatra."

Was she speaking about me or someone else?

25

Another "Only in New Orleans" thing was that the station was next to Café Beignet. Forget doughnuts, this city's police eat beignets. Surrounded by a wrought-iron fence, the stately building with two-story columns was the most attractive police station. Not that I had seen many and none from the inside.

If the row of motorcycles lined up didn't give it away, the sign on the front that said "NOPD T-SHIRTS AVAILABLE INSIDE STATION" did. After asking for the detectives, I wandered over to a vending machine which didn't dispense food, but had the aforementioned T-shirts. Did they sell that many that they needed a machine? Everything could be a souvenir in this city.

"I'll get you one after our meeting, if you like," Rob said as he walked over to me, offering his hand.

"Does everyone get one after they meet with detectives?"

"Shhhh, don't say that too loud. We don't need any more reports than we get now. You'd be amazed what tourists will do for free stuff," he whispered with a twinkle in his eyes.

Between their good looks, kindness, and sense of humor, Sissy and Rob were the perfect couple.

Detective Christine Gammon was waiting for us in a small conference room in the back of the building. She shook my hand and offered me a sturdy chair across the four-person Formica table. Between the utilitarian furniture and beige walls, it had to be the dullest room I'd ever walked into. If the interior decorator's purpose was to make people so bored that they had no choice but to focus on their statement, they succeeded.

"Coffee? We get it from Café Beignet. Police station coffee is as bad as you can imagine."

"No, thank you."

"Okay, let's start. First, we have some questions to go over, and then we'll have you write up your account. How does that sound?"

It sounded horrible, but I was sure that wasn't the right answer. I nodded, and we settled in our chairs and began. I retold the story without interruption from either of them.

"And then the police showed up, and you know the rest."

"Yes, we do, thanks. Miss Sammy, let's go over the time you saw the victim. The night before, correct?" Rob asked as he flipped through his notebook. "But you'd never seen her before?"

I nodded and was about to claim she probably wasn't looking for our group. It would have been a lie, but I felt that I should be loyal to my friends. Rob stopped me before I fibbed.

"Does the name Kelly Nelson sound familiar? Have you been to the Daiquiri Den?"

"No, to both questions," I said. Then it hit me. I looked from Detective Gammon to Rob. "Wait, her name was Kelly?"

"Yes. She's from Georgia and moved to New Orleans six months ago. According to her roommates, Kelly's been working at the bar on Bourbon since she got here."

Yesterday's nausea tried to return, but I breathed deeply to rid myself of it. I didn't want to show my confusion, but my shivering and deep breaths weren't hiding it.

"Miss Sammy, are you okay?" Rob asked as he went to the thermostat. "I'll warm up the room."

"Did you recognize her name?" Detective Gammon demanded. She was definitely the bad cop.

I shook my head and took one more deep breath. "I thought she was Sarah since that's the name on the card."

"I can see why you assumed that, but I wonder why you're so upset by the name," Detective Gammon said.

I wondered, too. My physical reaction to this information surprised me, too. "I guess it adds to the mystery. Why would someone put a card with the wrong name on it with her body?"

"That's a good question, but we don't have an answer for it...yet," Rob said.

"Do you know if any of the men with you the other night go to that bar? Have they mentioned it or Kelly?" Detective Gammon asked as she moved from the chair across from me to the one next to me. "Any information you can share, no matter how irrelevant it seems, might help us."

"No, they've never talked about a Kelly. I've only been to The Gas Light with them. And I meant it when I said I only saw her the night before," I snapped. My body was under control, and now I wanted to keep the situation in my control. As much as I could against two seasoned detectives.

"Miss Sammy, we believe you," Rob said as he patted my hand across the table while his partner frowned at him. "It's important we learn all we can about Kelly."

"I understand. How was she killed? When did she die?" I said, praying it happened during the party.

Rob opened up the folder in front of him. "We're waiting on the autopsy report, but it appears to be blunt force trauma. The preliminary time is between 1 a.m. and 6 a.m. Now, you know from TV shows that we have to ask you this as a formality. Where were you during those hours?"

"Home alone, and no, I didn't see anyone."

"Okay. Let's go back to the doll and note you found on the body. That reminds me, we'll need your fingerprints before you leave," Rob said. "Just to rule you out since you explored the house."

"Sorry about that," I said.

"Everyone touches things. You weren't expecting to find a body, were you?" Detective Gammon said with a smile, but I didn't think she was joking.

"No." I smiled back to play along. "I assumed I would discover more initials like I did when I followed the other entries. Did you find anything else in the diary?"

They looked at each other in the way longtime friends or partners do. "It's being analyzed right now," Detective Gammon said.

Damn. My hope was they would pull out the diary, so I could read the next pages. One of my many talents from being an administrative assistant was reading material upside down. No luck today.

They asked a few more questions, and then I wrote my official statement for them. A police woman took my fingerprints, and then Rob walked me out and offered a T-shirt again. I passed, but thanked him for his offer and making the process as easier than I expected.

"You're welcome, Miss Sammy. I hope this won't ruin your view on New Orleans. Sissy says you fit right in."

"I won't let it. I love New Orleans already. And bad things happen everywhere."

"That they do. Stay safe and we'll be in touch."

I believed bad things could happen everywhere, but hopefully I'd had my share of them in New Orleans.

26

I exited the building to find sunshine and jazz. Quite the contrast to the beige and seriousness of the last hours I spent inside the police station. The heaviness of the situation weighed on my body and mind as I leaned against the fence planning my next move. I couldn't just forget about yesterday.

Not that I didn't have confidence in Rob and his partner's abilities, but deep in my heart I knew this was more than a random murder. How did my following the diary's puzzles lead to Sarah's, I mean, Kelly's death? What did the BB dolls mean? And what did the key unlock?

My hopelessness required my usual quick fix, a coffee break. I joined the line at Café Beignet hoping caffeine would help me plan my next move. Beignets might help, too.

I wished I had the diary to see where the scavenger hunt continued to in the French Quarter. Could Sissy ask Rob to return it to me? No, I couldn't ask her to do that. There had to be a way to get it back. I should have asked the detectives for a copy.

Hold it, Andrew made a copy when I met him.

Thank goodness, or was there more to his actions than helpfulness? It didn't matter. I still had a shot at figuring out what happened.

Yes, I was on the case. I laughed out loud to the concern of a group of camera-laden tourists waiting in line with me. I'm sure Andrew wouldn't mind if I stopped by to read the rest of the book. Unless he was the writer of the diary.

Or the murderer.

I didn't laugh this time, but I was being ridiculous. I couldn't suspect every person I knew in New Orleans of murder.

Skipping the beignets, I ordered two café au laits. I assumed Andrew didn't welcome powdered sugar in his pristine bookshop and that's where I needed to go.

27

———————

The door to Lagniappe Books opened before I reached the first step. "My dear Samantha," Andrew said as he ushered me inside. "Libby told me what happened to you. I am so sorry."

He turned the sign to Closed, and then guided me to the back of the store. He motioned for me to sit in one chair while he sat in the other. "I'm glad you came to see me, as I was going to call you. Which reminds me; you need to contact Libby and Sissy at once. They're worried sick about you."

"Oh, you're right, I didn't text them after the police station. I'm sure Sissy has already called Rob for details," I said while texting them. "That is if Detective Gammon lets him speak."

Andrew's laugh filled the room and I couldn't help but join in. "So, you've figured out Rob and his relationships. He's a good man, and a great boyfriend to Sissy. I think she and his work partner keep him on his toes."

"I like all the strong women I've met so far. It must be a Southern thing."

"Very true," Andrew said. "The men aren't so bad either. Has Connor brought you more flowers?"

I tried to act casual, but the warmth in my cheeks and the involuntarily smile gave it away. "Yes, he did last night."

"I'm glad to hear it. You deserve a bit of cheer after the incident. I can't even imagine it."

"It was awful. I've read so many mysteries, but nothing prepared me for seeing an actual body." I reached for my coffee on the table to gather myself. "I'm not sure if it was just a coincidence or if it has something to do with the diary."

As I sipped my drink, I studied Andrew's face. I couldn't pin down his response. Was he curious? Was he sympathetic? Did he know more than he was saying?

"Well, I, for one, do not believe in coincidences. Is this coffee for me? How thoughtful. Is it café au lait?" He took a sip. "No beignets? I'm joking. You guessed I didn't partake of our official pastry?"

"Yes, I must admit I assumed you weren't a beignet-in-the-store kind of owner."

"You're correct, but I would make an exception for you. Now, let's talk about the diary. What did the police say?"

"They took it, but they haven't said a word about it." I felt compelled to tell him the whole story of finding the body and my discussion with the detectives. I left out the part about the woman appearing to recognize one of my friends. As much as I liked Andrew, I owed the guys some loyalty. I admitted I had seen Kelly the night before, but I didn't know her.

"It is a strange tale. I'm sure the police will solve it quickly. No one likes an unsolved murder in the Quarter, especially our mayor. In New Orleans, the only thing worse than an unsolved crime is a hurricane."

He looked away from me, and I noticed a slight shift in his energy. I wanted to ask him about his Katrina experience, but he perked up and started talking.

"While we shouldn't interfere with the detectives, it wouldn't hurt to review the diary once again. That was one reason you came here, isn't it? And to deliver coffee." His smile returned, and his eyes were looking at me in amusement.

"I'm happy to bring you café au lait anytime, but yes, I wanted to look over the copy since I don't have the original."

From a folder on the table, he pulled out a copy of the journal. Was I this predictable, or was Andrew hoping I would come by today?

"I looked through it, and it still reads as a bad romance novel. Do young women speak this way?" he asked as he handed the pages to me. "This doesn't sound like you or Sissy."

I agreed with him and flipped to the section about the shotgun cottage. I turned the page over. "Where is the rest?"

"That was all. Yes, I'm sure. The last entry was literally a dead end."

28

N o! This couldn't be the last page. Was I meant to find a body?

"I can see by your face you're shocked. You expected more entries?"

"Yes," I said after I settled back into the chair. "I assumed the book would end with a romantic proposal, not a murder."

"I did, too," Andrew said as he skimmed through the copy. "It makes me think the woman you found was, in fact, the writer. What do you know about her?"

"Only that her name is Kelly Nelson, and she worked at the Daiquiri Den."

"You have two options," he said as he put the papers back in the folder and handed it to me. "You can try to forget about the diary and the murder and leave it to the police..."

"And the other option?"

"Go to the Daiquiri Den and do a little investigating," he answered. "Discreetly, of course. I would come with you, but I think her coworkers will talk to you more than they would me."

"And I bet daiquiris aren't your drink." I smiled at him, but the seriousness of the situation hit me. "That's what I want to do. I can't forget the diary or the sight of Kelly wrapped in plastic."

"You have your answer, then. Just be careful."

"Before I leave, did you find anything about my key?"

"You kept it?"

I pulled the necklace out from under my shirt. "I forgot to mention it came with the journal to the detectives."

He raised an eyebrow at me and said, "On purpose, perhaps? No, don't tell me. I assume you tried it at the cottage?"

I nodded.

"I would keep it for the moment. Especially since I still haven't discovered what it opens yet. I emailed a photo to a friend, but he is out of town. Oh, now, don't worry, we will find the answer!"

My face must have shown my disappointment as Andrew pulled me gently out of my chair and hugged me. How could I have suspected he had anything to do with this mess? It was time to trust my friends again. Unless they proved otherwise.

"Thanks for listening and helping," I said as I gathered my belongings and headed to the front door. "I'll keep you posted on my investigations."

"Please do." He turned the store sign to Open. "I'll let you know as soon as I hear from my friend. Take care."

I felt hopeless and confused after my meeting at the police station. The situation was still puzzling, but I had a focus now. Time to get a daiquiri.

29

———

I left the busy yet calm atmosphere of Royal Street and walked to boisterous Bourbon Street. Even though it was early afternoon, the parties had already started. With cups in hand, tourists strolled up and down the road, going from bar to bar. Tonight it would be wall-to-wall of semi-drunk to completely inebriated partiers, but for now I could easily maneuver the crowds in search of the Daiquiri Den.

Smiling and saying "No, thanks" to the employees yelling to come and get a five-dollar beer, I found Kelly Nelson's workplace. I saw the square neon sign for the bar first, but the memorial in front confirmed it.

A plastic cup holding a mixed bouquet of white flowers was propped up against the wall in between two doors that opened into the building. I crouched down to stare at a photo of Kelly with two women about her age. Wearing fuchsia Daiquiri Den tank tops, they had their arms around each other, laughing into the camera. My heart broke for them.

I peered into the virtually empty bar. Kelly's friends were

the only people there. Behind the counter stood one woman, rubbing a nonexistent spill with a rag. The other woman hunched over the bar, her stool wobbling as she twirled a paper umbrella in a daiquiri cup.

Was it right to barge in on their grief? As I contemplated leaving, the bartender called out, "Hi. We're open. It's just a tough day, but we have two-for-one drinks in honor of our friend."

I stepped inside and sat a seat away from the seated woman. "I'll take a strawberry daiquiri."

Brittany, according to her name tag, placed the cups in front of me. Even with the techno music playing, and the flashing lights on the wall of daiquiri machines, the sense of loss overwhelmed me.

I handed her a twenty and left the change she returned on the counter. She took away her friend's now empty cup.

"Would you like my other drink?" I asked her once she lifted her head. The tears flowing from her bloodshot eyes mixed with the mucus from her reddened nose, but she didn't seem to notice or care. Brittany handed her a handful of napkins, so she got the hint and wiped her face.

"That's kind of you, but I shouldn't," the now clean woman replied. "I'll just start crying again."

"Losing a friend must be horrible."

"How did you know? Oh, you saw the memorial. I miss her so much." She sniffled as she reached for my offering. "To Kelly," she said as she lifted her drink in the air.

She and I raised our cups as did Brittany who now had her own daiquiri. Under the circumstances, I didn't think the bar owners would mind.

"Listen, I don't know how to say this," I said after taking a large sip of my strong cocktail. "I'm the one who found your friend yesterday."

The gasps from Kelly's friends cut through the loud music. Not knowing what to do, I babbled on, "I'm sorry. I'm intruding, but I wanted to pay my respects." And ask questions.

"You should have told me that first," Brittany said. She turned around and opened the register.

I stood up and grabbed my backpack to leave. What an idiot I was to waltz in here to question these women like the police. I wasn't even a good amateur detective. I made it a few steps when Brittany called out.

"Here's your money. The drinks are on me."

Her friend stumbled off her stool and pulled me back to the bar. "Thank you for finding Kelly. She's gone, but at least she wasn't missing for long."

"Trish is right. It could have been days or weeks before someone found her. We're glad you did." Brittany rushed to the other end of the bar to help a gaggle of tourists who bounded in, oblivious to the seriousness of our conversation.

"How did she look? Did she suffer?" Trish pleaded as tears began dripping down her face again.

"She looked like an angel," I said. "I'm sure she didn't suffer." Which might be a lie, but I hoped that she died instantly.

"Thanks," she said as she used her last napkin to wipe her face.

"I wish I could tell you more. The police didn't share much with me."

"Same here. They came to our apartment to give us the news and then kicked us out to search it. Not cool."

I put my arm around Trish's shoulders to keep her from falling backward off her stool. "That's awful. Did they find anything?"

"They took her laptop and asked about her cell phone. It's missing."

"I'm sure they'll figure it out soon," I said as I finished my drink. I now regretted giving my second one to Trish, but she needed it more than I did.

"They better," Trish yelled and then slapped the counter with both hands. "I know what happened to her."

"You do?"

"It had to be that guy she's been seeing."

"You mean the mystery man?" Brittany said as she returned. "He really seemed to like her."

"You met him?" I asked.

"No," she said. "Kelly said he was shy. I thought he was married."

"Did she say what his name was? Or what he looked like?"

"It was strange," Brittany answered. "She called him 'my guy' and told us he was tall, dark, and handsome. She was so secretive about him to the point of being annoying. But she was happy, so we just dealt with it."

"Hey." Trish turned to me. "Why were you in there? The cops said it was under construction. Do you own it?"

"Um, no." I gulped the dregs of my drink. "This will sound crazy, but I found a diary in my new apartment, and I followed the riddles to different parts of the Quarter. The house was the last place."

I decided not to tell them about the key, the dolls, or the "RIP Sarah" note. No need to confuse them any more than they were.

"Whose diary was it?" Brittany asked as she placed another drink in front of each of us.

"I thought it might be Kelly's. Would it be too much to ask you both to look at it?"

"You have it?" they exclaimed.

"I gave the original to the police, but I have a copy. I'm not trying to interfere, but you can imagine how curious I am."

Brittany came around the bar and sat next to Trish. They huddled over the diary, reading each page slowly. It was torturous waiting for them to finish the book. I twirled my umbrella and watched as their expressions moved from confusion to annoyance. Trish handed it back to me with a scowl on her face.

"It's not Kelly's handwriting, and she didn't talk like that. It's not her diary."

30

Feeling as if I'd just finished a marathon only to be told it didn't count, I sat there stunned. After Kelly's friends said she had a mystery man, I assumed she was the diary writer. It would explain why she was at that house, but it didn't explain her murder.

"I hate to ask, but are you positive? Could she have done it as a present to her boyfriend?"

Brittany answered first: "She liked romance, but she didn't read them and she wouldn't have written one."

"She said she went to a bunch of places in the Quarter with that guy, but I can't see her keeping a diary like that one," Trish said as her eyes welled up again. "She didn't even write Facebook posts."

"Oh." I tried not to sigh, but it came out.

"You think the diary and Kelly's murder are related?" Brittany asked. Trish looked annoyed about the whole situation. Or her third daiquiri was kicking in.

"Maybe. It's just strange that she had a mystery man, and I had a diary that led to her."

"That guy did it. The police better find him because if I

find him first…" Trish sputtered before dropping her head and sobbing.

A man in a Daiquiri Den T-shirt rushed past the tourists, hurrying out the door. "Hey, Trish, it's okay." He gave her heaving shoulders a hug and then joined Brittany behind the bar.

"Thank God you're here, Brian. I need to take her home, and honestly, I don't think I can work my whole shift," Brittany said as she gave Brian a quick embrace.

"Yeah, you need to take Trish home and stay with her. Thanks for working until I got here. Call me later and let me know how y'all are doing," Brian said as he cleaned off the empty cups on the bar. "And I'll find some people to cover your shifts tomorrow."

"Thanks, and hey, did you meet Kelly's boyfriend?"

"No, she never brought him here," Brian said. "I'm sorry this happened to her. She was a sweet kid."

Trish started crying again, so Brittany took her hand and pulled her out the door. I grabbed a few napkins but left my money on the counter for Brian. I followed the women to the sidewalk. Not wanting to intrude any more on their grief, I scribbled my contact information on a napkin.

"Here's my number if I can help or if you remember something. I'm so sorry," I whispered to Brittany. She nodded her head, and she and Trish began walking home away from the bar.

The amateur detective in me wanted to follow them and go through Kelly's room, but I stopped myself. I wouldn't find anything the police hadn't already found. While she had a mystery man, I had no proof it was the man in the diary. And now I knew Kelly didn't write it. But who did? And why?

31

———————

My head ached along with my heart as I pictured Brittany and Trish heading to their apartment without their friend. I believed them when they declared Kelly didn't write the journal, but I was positive it involved her. It was too much of a coincidence that she had a mystery man who took her around the French Quarter like the diary writer. And I've never known a woman to not talk about her new boyfriend unless there was an issue.

Why did the diary end up in my apartment? Was it for me or was it another coincidence? If I hadn't found it or not followed the puzzles, would Kelly be alive? I owed it to her, and to myself, to find out why this happened. But for now, I needed to forget about the murder and remember why I moved to New Orleans. And for that, I went to Jackson Square.

Even with the tourists, artists, psychics, musicians, and strangely painted mimes, it was a refreshing break from reality. With the area filled with ordinary people to amazing performers to mysterious fortune tellers, it was a good reminder of the positive energy and quirkiness of the neighborhood. By sitting in the park and tapping my toes to the brass band performing in front of the historical buildings, this would be the place to come to clear my head.

When the music ended, I walked over to the church. St. Louis Cathedral stood out with its arches, columns, and three steeples topping the substantial building. I couldn't decide whether to go in or wait another day when the bells rang four times. I decided to head home, but then I recognized a voice behind me.

"Now, here we are at the elegant and inspiring St. Louis Cathedral. Yes, it's named after King Louis IX of France. The church has been in this spot since the early 1700s, but the one we're looking at today was built in 1850. Hey, Sammy! Come join us!"

There was no hiding from Neal and his group of a dozen tourists now standing next to me. He gave me a quick hug and put a tour sticker on my shirt. Like Sissy last night, he wasn't taking no for an answer.

"Hi," I said as all eyes were on me. "If you don't mind, I'll tag along."

"Of course not! Folks, this is my new friend and neighbor, Sammy. She needs to learn this city if she's going to live here, right?"

The crowd nodded in agreement while smiling at Neal. His charm worked on everyone. He continued speaking, and the group focused on him once again.

Joey came over to me and said, "Hey, how are you doing today? Yesterday must have been rough."

"I'm fine," I lied. "I'm trying not to think about it." I didn't want to let him or any of the other guys know I would keep researching the diary. They were all suspects, but I still had a hard time believing it.

"Glad you're all right. If you need to talk, I'm here for you."

"Thanks. Why are you on the tour? Brushing up on your New Orleans history for school?"

"I'm shadowing the tours so I can be a backup guide. Or maybe even join the company."

He looked over at Matt who shrugged. "Yeah, I understand y'all need more business for that to happen." Joey left us to stand with Neal.

Matt whispered as we entered the sanctuary, "Neal is the showman on our tours. I follow in the back and make sure we don't lose anyone. It's usually on the nighttime tour that I have to wrangle some tipsy tourists. The daytime ones are tamer."

"He enjoys it, doesn't he?" I said as we listened to Neal explain the church's history. "Seems like you're busy. And you have Joey who wants to work for you."

"Neal is a history fanatic with a love of show business. That helps us a lot. It's competitive here. You need a hook to get the tourists, and then you need good word of mouth to keep it going," Matt said, but stopped talking to smile as I paused at the entry of the sanctuary.

The exterior of the cathedral was impressive, but the inside was the real showstopper. The black-and-white, diamond-patterned tile floor grounded the room as detailed paintings and stained-glass windows covered the walls and ceilings. Country flags hanging from the balconies surprised me, but it added to my belief that New Orleans was an international city. The influences of other countries were clear in the food, architecture, music, and in the church.

Matt spoke again after we passed a lone woman praying in a pew. "It's amazing here, isn't it? Well, back to the business. We're doing okay, not enough to hire Joey. He's not ready for this job, anyway."

"I don't know history, but I know social media. I was serious about my offer the other day."

"That's really kind of you, especially after all that's happened to you," Matt said as we followed the group to the racks of votive candles outside the sanctuary doors. "Our office is unorganized right now. Give me a day or two to put the place in order a bit, and then I'll have you come over. I'd appreciate your help. I don't want to lose this business."

And with that statement, Matt pushed a dollar into the box next to the candles and lit one. Joey joined us and did the same. Although I wasn't Catholic, I copied them, but paid for three candles. One for my mom, my dad, and Kelly.

"Who are you lighting candles for, if you don't mind me asking?" Joey asked after I opened my eyes from saying a prayer for them all. I wasn't sure if that was part of the process, but it felt right.

"For my parents and for the woman I found yesterday."

"I'm sure your folks will appreciate that. Is your family Catholic?"

"No, we didn't go to church. I think my parents would welcome the gesture anyway."

"I bet they would. Matt, who are you lighting a candle for today?"

Matt opened his eyes and said with a slight smile, "Isn't this like blowing out candles on your birthday? You're not supposed to say or your wish won't come true."

"I'll have to check with a priest about that." Joey laughed quietly as we walked out of the cathedral.

I begged off the rest of the tour, with exhaustion as my excuse. I promised to meet the guys the next night at The

Gas Light. Hopefully, an early dinner and bedtime would put me back in order.

As I entered the courtyard, I found Sissy sitting at my outdoor table with her phone in her hand.

"I was just about to call you. I brought dinner from my momma. She insisted I come home to tell her what happened, and she sent me home with food." Sissy followed me in as I opened my door. "And I pulled some information out of Rob about the murder."

She put the stack of containers on the counter and spun to face me. "And I have some news about you."

32

"About me? I promise I've never been arrested. My credit is good."

Sissy laughed and hugged me. "I know! Well, I don't know about the credit, but Rob says you don't have a criminal history."

She sat me down on the couch and opened a bottle of wine in the kitchen. "What I mean is Rob has the paperwork from when they found you as a toddler after Hurricane Geoffrey. You might already have this info, though."

I took a swig from the wineglass Sissy handed me. I went to my bedroom and brought out one document. "This is all I have."

"This is it?" She raised the birth certificate issued on my adoption date. "Your parents didn't give you any other papers? Okay then, what did they tell you about your origins?"

"They said the police found me on the Louisiana side of I-55 near the Mississippi border. I was sitting by the freeway, crying and holding on to that doll." I pointed to my BB doll on the shelf. "They took me to the hospital where they decided I was around two, based on my size and limited speech. All I said was Sam, so they assumed my name was Samantha."

"That confirms the police reports," Sissy said as she opened up her phone. "Rob wouldn't let me copy the papers, so I took a few notes."

"Why am I not surprised? I'm sure you can pry info out of anyone, especially him."

"I have my ways. He didn't want to tell me anything without talking to you first, but everything he has is public record. Did you know you can request information from the Department of Child and Family Services?"

I shook my head.

"So, anyway, Christine called Rob out of his office, and he left the papers on his desk," she said. "I was shocked they never put your story out to other states besides Louisiana. I can't believe they didn't search for your family in Mississippi or Alabama. Or even Texas on a long shot. Did you know that?"

"No. My parents told me they took me in as a foster child in Baton Rouge. Once they adopted me, we moved to Florida. They never wanted to talk about my adoption, so I gave up asking."

"Oh." Sissy took a moment, then asked, "What do you think happened to your family? Do you recall anything at all?"

"I have no idea and no memories. I went to Café du Monde the other day to see if I would remember something from the photograph."

"And?"

"Nothing came to me. Maybe I'm wrong about the picture. The date could be a misprint."

"You don't believe that, do you?"

"No, but it makes no sense. Why was I in the city as a child? If I lived here, some family members would have claimed me."

"They might have all died, honey," Sissy said. "But listen to what Rob found."

As exhausted as I was, Sissy's enthusiasm for my past kept me listening.

"Let me read this part that I wrote down from a social worker's report at the home they first put you in. 'Child is comfortable with adults, but searches the rooms for older children. She gravitates toward picture books that show families and is fond of the book *Beads, Beignets, and Bobby at Mardi Gras.*' It also said you were well-behaved, but hated naps."

"*Beads, Beignets, and Bobby at Mardi Gras*? I guess I've always liked a party."

"Sammy, don't you see? I bet you're from New Orleans," Sissy insisted. "Even a stranger picked up on your interest in New Orleans! You were drawn to the city, weren't you?"

"Yes, I love books and movies about the city. And I'm comfortable here, but that's the people."

"I agree the people here are great, but come on! You must be a New Orleans native!"

"I hope you're right, and I appreciate the information," I said. "You're doing more research on my adoption than me. Thank you."

"You're welcome! That's what friends are for, and let's face it, you've been a bit distracted. What do you want to do next about it?"

Before I could answer, there was a knock on the door. I was glad for the reprieve as I needed time to consider my plans. I had more information tonight than I'd ever had, but it still didn't confirm I was born or lived in New Orleans.

Sissy opened the door and let Neal and Joey inside.

"Good evening, ladies. We saw the light on, so we wanted to check on our resident body finder," Neal said while leaning down to kiss my cheek. "Just joking! Sissy, is that your mom's gumbo I smell?"

"Where's Matt?" I asked.

"He's upstairs already," Joey said after giving me a hug. "He said he was exhausted and would see y'all tomorrow."

Neal beelined to the kitchen. "Oh, man, that smells so good! Not as good as my momma's, but not bad at all." He and Joey helped themselves and sat on the floor by us.

"My momma makes the best gumbo. One day we'll get our moms together for a cook-off," Sissy said as she packed the rest of the food in my fridge.

"Where do your parents live, Neal?" I asked.

"They're in Alabama now. We lived in Mississippi when I was little, but we moved when I was in high school."

"Is that where you met Matt?"

"No, we met at Ole Miss, which is the University of Mississippi to you. Have you been to Oxford yet? We need to take you to a game. As long as Sissy won't cry when her team loses."

"You'll be the one crying," Sissy said as she took the empty bowls and spoons and washed them. "I like the idea of us going to a game."

"Let's do it! We could even invite Andrew and Connor. Sammy seems to bring the best out of them."

That was sweet of Neal to say, but I wasn't sure it was true. I connected with both of them easily, but I wonder if they both weren't ready to make some changes, and I just came along at the right time.

"Joey, where did you go to college?" I asked.

"Mississippi State."

"So, you're a bulldog," Sissy said.

"Yep," Joey said. "That was a long time ago, though."

"What are you now as a grad student?" I said.

"Um, a bird, I think." Joey laughed. "I don't follow sports in grad school."

"Too busy studying?" Sissy asked.

"Too busy hanging out with us." Neal slapped Joey on the back. "I don't know how you do grad school and party with us."

"I'm just a multitasker," Joey said. "You know, like how you can ride a skateboard and drink a beer. I'm just that talented."

We all laughed and life felt normal for a moment. Then Neal asked, "Hey, you might not want to talk about yesterday, but did you find out anything about the woman who was killed?"

"You're right, she doesn't want to talk about it," Sissy said.

"It's okay," I said. "I did learn she worked at the Daiquiri Den. Have you been there?"

"I probably have. All those bars look the same on Bourbon," Neal said. Joey nodded in agreement. "Did Rob share any more?"

"He's not giving me anything else just yet. I'll keep you posted," Sissy promised.

"Sounds good. Thanks for the food. And, hey, I hoped you liked the tour," Neal said. "See you at The Gas Light tomorrow, okay? Keep your chin up, Sammy. New Orleans is crazy, but you shouldn't find any more bodies."

He and Joey hugged me before leaving. We could hear their laughter as they raced up the steps to Neal and Matt's apartment. I hope Matt enjoyed a little peace and quiet before they got there.

"Neal's right, things will be calmer. Well, after Mardi Gras they will," Sissy said as she finished cleaning up my kitchen and pulled me off the couch. "Bedtime, young lady. Tomorrow's a new day."

"Thanks for everything. I appreciate how much you're helping. And thank Rob for the info. I'll give it some thought."

"You do that, honey. Maybe you'll find out where you came from because of all this. Wouldn't that be something?"

Yes, it would be something, but for now all I wanted was my bed. I drifted to sleep with thoughts of beignets and beads dancing in my head.

33

The insistent buzzing of my cell phone woke me out of my Mardi Gras parade dream. I managed to say "Hello?" instead of "Throw me something, mister!"

"There was a murder in your neighborhood, and I saw a picture of you at the crime scene! I'd recognize the back of your head anywhere. Why didn't you call me? What's going on there?"

"Good morning, Madeline. I guess Athena woke up early."

"Yes, as she usually does. You're not still in bed, are you? That's not like you. What is happening to you?"

"After the past few days, I needed my sleep." And with that I filled my San Francisco best friend in on the events of late. I left out the part about my concerns that one of my friends knew the victim. I didn't want to add to the anxiety I could hear in her voice.

"Samantha, you could have been killed! I don't know what to say, except you need to be careful. Or better yet, come back home!"

Home? San Francisco wasn't home anymore. New Orleans was home even with all the craziness.

"I promise I'll be careful. Hopefully, they'll find the killer soon and this will all be part of the past. I can use the experience to write a mystery like I wanted to do in college."

"While I'm all for you becoming a famous author, I'd prefer you to be safe. What about the diary? Is it connected to you or is it some weird coincidence? Either way, I don't like it."

"I'm not sure, but I'll put it aside for now and go back to exploring museums and shops," I lied.

"Okay. I feel a little better. Everyone's asking about you, so you need to update your Facebook status. Let's see more pictures!"

Madeline's daughter dumping her cereal on the floor ended our conversation, but not before I promised to be careful and work on my social media accounts.

After a quick shower, I grabbed my backpack and headed to Royal Street to take photos as Madeline demanded. I wandered for a few blocks, snapping pictures of a few balconies dripping with ferns until I couldn't ignore my growling stomach. Libby's café was close by, so I made my way through the early morning crowds to find breakfast.

As usual, the line was long, but Libby spotted me right away. "Sammy! Sit down and I'll bring you coffee and a scone."

I did as she said and picked a table in the back next to an open window. I needed the crisp air to keep me awake while I waited for my coffee. While waiting, I took out the copy of the diary and reread it. I opened up my notebook and scribbled a list of the places I went to:

Napoleon House
Mardi Gras Museum
Cottage on Bourbon Street

I WROTE KEY, doll, and Sarah and circled them on the page. I was drawing a big question mark when Libby walked up with my coffee and a cranberry scone.

"Still thinking about the diary? Honey, let the police handle it."

"I will, but it's hard not to think about it," I said and then sipped my café au lait. "It's just so strange. Was it a coincidence that I found the book? Did anyone else look at the apartment before I did? Maybe it was for them?"

Libby shook her head and sat down at the table. "No, you were the first and only person I showed the place to after Mark moved out."

I wanted her opinion on Sissy's theory I was originally from New Orleans, so I recounted our conversation from the night before. For a moment her face expressed concern, but then she smiled widely.

"Oh, sweetie, aren't you reaching just a bit? You might be from anywhere in Louisiana." She patted my hand. "Bless your heart, your family might have been tourists visiting here. Sissy means well, but I'm not sure that's your story."

I nodded and took a big bite out of my scone to stop myself from arguing with her. Not that she was necessarily wrong. It was a stretch to assume I was born and raised in New Orleans before the hurricane turned the state upside down. It changed my life, but where did my life start? The picture I had could have been from a visit to New Orleans, not from living here. But it still didn't answer the question why it was hidden from me.

Libby rushed off to help her staff as another wave of customers entered the café. I lost my appetite, so I pushed my food aside and took one more glance at my notebook. I slapped it shut and put it away in my backpack. I planned to forget about the mystery of my birth, but a man's voice wouldn't let me.

"Samantha, darling, don't be sad. I believe you're on the way to finding out who you are."

34

———

"Come walk me to my shop. You need a sympathetic ear."

Andrew stood outside the window. Seeing his kind blue eyes and welcoming smile, he was the friend I needed. I gathered my notebook and backpack and I slinked out of the café, hoping I wouldn't catch Libby's attention.

"I hate to be an eavesdropper. I was about to say hello when I overheard you sharing your story with Libby," Andrew said after giving me a long hug when I met him on the street. "Sissy is always trying to fix things, and Libby prefers life without conflict, so I'm not surprised by either of them."

"They both mean well, but I really want the truth about my birth family. It's become more than a curiosity," I said.

"Besides your parents' passing, is there anything else motivating your search?"

I stared at Andrew, trying to decide if he was guessing or he actually knew I was hiding something. Deciding I could trust him, like Sissy, I took out the photo from my wallet.

"I found this hidden in my mother's desk after they died.

It was taken months before the hurricane. They always claimed they knew nothing about my life before my adoption."

Andrew removed the picture from my hand and studied it. He looked up and down at me and the photograph. He then handed the photo back to me.

"I understand now. Your parents had more information, it seems, and that was a confusing and painful revelation."

"Yes, that describes it. I'm still processing it a year later, but I'm determined to find the answers."

"You don't give up easily, do you? Including solving your diary mystery?"

"That's true. The fact the diary was in my apartment, and the BB dolls showed up at my house and the crime scene, is too much of a coincidence. And who is Sarah?"

"And don't forget the key," Andrew said. "You have several mysteries in your life."

"It's not what I expected to find when I moved here, to say the least."

"The diary is strange enough, but finding a body from it, well, that is crazy even by New Orleans' standards."

We both laughed for a moment, stopping to enjoy the joyful sounds of a trumpet player. When the song ended, he continued. "Many people, including myself, move here searching for something missing from their life. For me, I discovered love. You appear to be heading down a path of knowledge."

"I'm heading down some path, but I don't know if it's leading to my past or my present, or both. All I know is that I love this city and the friends I've made here. It feels like home."

"I'm glad to hear that, but be careful. Letting people into your life and learning about yourself are necessary evils, I'm afraid. Don't give me that look like I'm crazy." He smiled, but his face grew serious again. "What I mean is being part of a community, of a family, has its price. Guard your relationships because when you lose them, it's heartbreaking."

Andrew stopped in front of his shop and hugged me gently. As I tried to take in all his words, he stepped out of our embrace and unlocked the door.

"Samantha, I know what I've lost. You don't. I wonder which is worse."

And with that Andrew escaped into his world of books while I stood on the sidewalk wondering if I was ready for the truth about my past and my future. I might not have a choice.

35

———

My conversation with Andrew weighed on me as I meandered through the Quarter. I didn't find any answers on my walk, but I found a quirky stationery store where I stocked up on writing supplies. Unblemished notepads and free-flowing pens would be a good motivator to work on my blog.

When I returned to my apartment, I warmed up the left-over gumbo and opened up one of my new notebooks. I doodled more than wrote in it. My mind had a hard time focusing. When Connor's text came through, it was a welcome distraction.

HEY. Slammed at work. Hope you're OK.

I'm good. Thanks. Eating gumbo from Sissy's mom.

Lucky! Not as tasty as mine though. I'll cook for you soon. Gotta run.

. . .

I CLOSED MY NOTEBOOK. The image of Connor cooking for me couldn't compete with describing muffulettas for a blog. I tried reading to take my mind off my current situation, but *Murder on the Orient Express* didn't work. Although I love every Agatha Christie book, this wasn't the best choice for someone trying not to think about the past.

I gave up reading and curled up on the love seat for a nap, a luxury I wouldn't always be able to indulge in. My savings and inheritance would last awhile, but eventually I needed to come up with a career plan. This wasn't the time as I succumbed to my heavy eyelids and napped.

I dreamt of walking through a cemetery, searching for gravestones marked Sarah. When I fell into an open grave, I yelled, waking myself up. A beam of light from the courtyard was enough for me to realize I was on my couch. I sat up and grabbed my buzzing cell phone. A text from Neal came through:

Gas Light at 9:30 Join the land of the living again.

Little did Neal know I just woke from the dead. My friend didn't seem worried about my emotional state after discovering a body, but he meant well. I texted him back.

I might be a zombie tonight, but I'll be there

Remembering the stale peanuts at the bar, I finished the gumbo and freshened up for the evening out. I was still tired, but a quick beer with friends sounded good.

Thinking I would enjoy a drama-free night, two people yelling in front of The Gas Light ruined my plans. I wasn't joining the land of the living, but the land of arguing roommates and business partners.

36

———

Neal and Matt were in a full-blown fight with their voices echoing off the surrounding buildings. This was more intense than the argument I witnessed a few nights ago.

"I've told you I'll try to help more, so can you just let it go? You're acting like my mother."

"I'm acting like an adult, Neal. If you don't stop giving away tours to girls you're trying to hook up with, we will go broke."

Neal's face turned red as he poked Matt's chest with his middle finger. "I did it a few times to drum up business, not get laid. If you tried to bring in business for us instead of hiding under paperwork, maybe you'd understand how hard it is for me."

"Hiding under paperwork? You don't have a clue how much work I do. You think it's all fun and games, but I'm the one keeping us going. Screw you." Matt's anger matched Neal's.

Their stances reminded me of bulls waiting to charge in a bullfight. Neither had the calmness of a matador; both were the animals. I stood like a spectator, horrified by what would come next. From what I'd seen of Neal, I assumed he would move first, but Matt's scowling face and clenched fists changed my mind. Before I could decide if I should intercede, they each took two steps backward.

"You know what, Neal, I'm over it for tonight." Matt lowered his voice. "I'm going to hide under some paperwork and we'll talk tomorrow when you're ready to be an adult. Or at least when you're sober."

He stormed off while Neal yelled after him, "Fine, asshole!"

Matt gave a one-finger response and picked up his pace. As he started to turn the corner, he ran into Joey.

"Sorry, dude, didn't mean to run into you. The bar is the other direction."

"I'm going to work, unlike some people," Matt snapped. "Go get drunk with your buddy, Joey, like you two always do."

"Go be the martyr, Saint Matt," Neal yelled as he stomped out of view.

"Whoa, what's up with him tonight?" Joey asked. "Oh, hi, Sammy."

Neal turned around, his face red from embarrassment I assumed. I could smell the beer on his breath and felt the tension in his body as he hugged me.

"Hey, did you hear that? I'm sorry, but don't worry." Neal smiled but his eyes told me otherwise. "Matt and I do that all the time. We're like an old married couple, I swear."

"What's that show with the mismatched roommates? *The Odd Couple*!" Joey laughed.

"I'm the messy one. Oscar, right?"

"Yes, and Matt is Felix," Joey said while opening the door.

Rose already had our beers waiting for us at the bar. Apparently the argument carried inside. "Hi, Sammy. Don't worry about our boys, they fight like brothers."

"Yep, that's us." Neal sighed. "Blood brothers until Matt becomes my dad. And my mom. I'm not an idiot."

"No, but listen to Matt more often," Rose spoke over Joey who was trying to defend Neal. "He always has your back."

Neal mumbled something under his breath, but stopped when he saw Rose's face. Her eyebrows had more expression than anyone I'd ever met. He nodded his head and was quiet.

"I promised to help you out with social media, but I'll add counseling to my list of things to do," I said as I squeezed Neal's hand. He pressed back and drank half his beer in one gulp.

"I thought we should just put them in those blow-up sumo wrestler costumes and let them duke it out," Joey said.

Neal laughed like his usual self. "Sounds good! Let's sell tickets. Connor, you'll buy one, right?"

Our neighbor joined us at the bar. Looking at Connor, I must have blushed as Joey winked at me. I ignored him and hoped Connor hadn't noticed.

"I'll buy tickets for the whole building," Connor said. "Thanks, Rose, here's my card. Put the drinks on my tab tonight."

"Will do, except for Sammy," Rose said as she snatched Connor's credit card. "Terry's already bought her drinks."

Terry walked over to the bar and gave Rose a handful of bills. "Her drinks are on me. Need to make sure she knows this is a good place, even if you find the dead among the living."

"Oh, you heard about it."

"Yes, cher, the construction foreman told me," he said

while patting me on the shoulder. "Next time you want to look at a house, you ask me. I'll check for bodies first."

He gave a toothless grin and chuckled as he sauntered out the door. The guys and Rose were laughing as they looked at my puzzled face.

"I'll take his drinks, but why did he call me what sounded like sha?"

"Cher is Cajun for dear," Rose said as she pulled another beer for Neal. "Terry is a sweetheart. He only means well."

"I have competition," Connor whispered in my ear. I sipped my beer instead of telling him that he didn't have any rivals.

People started crowding the bar, so Neal walked us to a table. The conversation flowed as did the beer. Around 11:30 p.m., I yawned louder than I meant to.

"Okay, I think Sammy is done tonight," Joey said. "I need to head out. Want me to walk you home?"

"I can do it. Are you ready, Sammy?" Connor said while pulling my chair back for me.

"Thanks for a fun evening. I needed it," I said after giving Joey and Neal each a quick kiss on the cheek. "Neal, do you want to come with us?"

"No, I'll stay for a bit, but thanks."

I hated leaving him there, but I assumed he was avoiding Matt who was probably home by now.

"See y'all soon." Joey waved goodbye and went in the opposite direction.

"How are you holding up?" Connor asked as we strolled back to our building.

"I'm fine, I guess. It's been a difficult experience."

"I know my momma feels bad you're mixed up in all this."

"That's kind of her," I said, but had to bite my tongue not

to tell him that his mother wasn't concerned about hurting my feelings this morning. Was that just me projecting my confusion about my past? Libby meant well, didn't she?

"You're already one of the family to my parents. We care about you." He put his arm around me and squeezed me gently. "Some of us more than others."

I let out another uncontrollable yawn instead of telling him I liked some people more than others, too.

Connor laughed. "You've got a great yawn. Seems like you still have some sleeping to catch up on. Me, too." He opened my door for me, kissed me on the cheek and said good night.

I needed to take a chance. I liked Connor, and after the craziness of the past few days I didn't want to be alone. Now was the time to invite him in for drinks or coffee or perhaps a little affection. I expected to see him enter his section of the building by the door in the courtyard.

Instead, I saw him walking out the front gate. I rushed back to my apartment and quietly closed my door. I leaned against it and exhaled all my disappointment. It wasn't the first time I'd misread a man's interest. Mixed in with my embarrassment and sadness was curiosity. Where was Connor heading that he didn't want me to know?

37

My tossing and turning in bed kept me from sleeping in like I did yesterday. Doubts about Connor still filled my head from last night. He didn't have to tell me where he was going after he walked me to my door. He owed me nothing; I wasn't his girlfriend.

Trying to forget him and focus on me, I threw off my covers and put on my running clothes at once. No excuse not to run now. I made a cup of coffee while I searched for my headphones and shoes. While sipping my drink, I created a new New Orleans-themed playlist that included music from Trombone Shorty and the Preservation Hall Jazz Band.

I found Cleopatra and her sister, Nefertiti, lounging in the courtyard when I stepped outside. As I stretched to warm up, the cats circled in and out of my legs. I laughed at them and myself as we distracted each other with our movements. "You both are cute, but you can't keep me from my run," I had to tell them or I would have never left. The thought of grabbing another cup of coffee, sitting at my outdoor table while petting the adorable kitties was tempting. I gave them one last scratch on their soft furry heads and jogged out the gate.

Royal Street was quiet at 7 a.m. The cool air pushed me to pick up my pace. It was a treat to run on flat roads after the hills of San Francisco. The thrill didn't continue as I ran up to Bourbon Street for a change of scenery. The remnants of the previous evening lingered. Repugnant smells assaulted my nose as the cleaners hosed down the sidewalks and roads. They were washing down the sweet stickiness of a night of fun, music, and perhaps even romance. The piles of trash, overwhelming stench, and half-empty to-go cups made me think otherwise.

I managed a few blocks of Bourbon Street but picked up my pace to turn down Ursuline to return to Royal. Matt and Neal's office was close by, so I kept going to check it out before I met them there later. I spotted their business's bright yellow sign hanging ahead. I popped up the stairs to see if their space reflected Matt's organizational skills or Neal's outgoing personality. When I pressed my face against the door's window to get a better look, I was surprised to find it was open.

I didn't expect them to be at work this early, but I couldn't imagine they would leave the door unlocked all night. Stepping inside, I called out, "Matt? Neal? Are you here?"

Someone designed the place to have the customers in and out quickly with only four stools on either side of a wooden podium that held the New Orleans Past & Present flyers. An open laptop sat on top of it with the retro Flying Toasters screensaver filling the screen. Framed newspaper articles and pictures of the guys with smiling tour groups lined the walls. It wasn't a terrible office, but it didn't represent Neal and Matt to the fullest. Besides social media, I would help them add a bit of pizazz to their waiting room.

In the back, a door marked Private was the only other place to search for them. I knocked and called out, "Hey, guys? It's Samantha. I mean, Sammy."

No answer. The stillness made me shiver. I wanted to leave the building and go call Matt and Neal from my phone outside. That would have been the logical thing to do, but logic hadn't been my strong suit these past days.

I turned the knob to find a small office with a desk, a chair, and two shelves with empty boxes. I assumed they held the business flyers that now covered the floor. It was a sea of papers; it reminded me of the aftermath of a storm.

Or a fight.

Did Neal and Matt continue their argument here? I took a step into the room, looking behind the door to check if the mess continued. I spotted a baseball bat propped up in the corner. The guys must use Mr. Gregory's choice of weapon for their office protection. The shiny wooden bat didn't appear to have been used much, and I wouldn't have given it a second thought if I hadn't noticed the smear of red paint on the top of it.

No. No. No.

Blood again? My breathing quickened as I stumbled backward and hit the door behind me, closing it with a bang. I regained my footing, but not my composure. Nausea, like the other day, returned, and my face was hot. I tiptoed on the flyers on the floor to get away from the bat. I didn't see anyone in the area. I should have just left, but I had to know if it was a murder weapon.

Gingerly moving around the room, I felt nothing underneath my feet. I finally checked behind the desk. With my next step in, I landed on a bulge under the papers. As I took my foot off the lump, the flyers scattered, and I saw what I stepped on. It was another shoe, but this time it wasn't a red high heel, but a well-worn tennis shoe attached to a large male foot.

No!

Common sense said to leave and call the police, but I lost any common sense I had. I brushed the rest of the papers off the body until I got to the top. My shaking hands hovered over the head, and with a deep breath, I uncovered the flyers.

The sticky papers fell to the side as did my heart. Blood-matted brown hair partially covered his face, but I recognized him. The kind eyes stared at me, making me think for a minute he was alive. I couldn't suppress my pain any longer, and I screamed the name of my neighbor, my friend who was dead.

38

"**M**att!"

I screamed his name, but he didn't move. I crouched down next to his face and pleaded, "Matt, please wake up. Please."

My brain understood he was dead, but I still reached out to touch his neck to check for a pulse. I jumped backward after my fingers touched his cool, stiff skin.

"What happened?" I whispered to his lifeless body after I focused on catching my breath. Finding a body a few days ago didn't prepare me for this, especially since he was a friend.

I needed to get help, so I wiped my tears and tried to go to the waiting room. My feet wouldn't move. While I couldn't do anything for him, I didn't want Matt to be alone.

I opened the office door but stayed inside to dial 9-1-1. I called Sissy next. "I-I need you at Matt and Neal's office," I stammered as she answered the phone. "Please come now."

"Sammy, what's going on? Okay, don't cry. I'm on my way," she said. "Rob, we need to go!" I heard her yell before she hung up. She was the right person to call for many reasons, the first being she was my closest friend here, and second, I knew she would be calm no matter what.

And I was correct. Sissy and Rob arrived at the same time as two uniformed police officers. She raced past them to find me in the office doorway.

"Sammy! What's going on? Oh my God." She stopped talking as her eyes grew wide upon seeing Matt's body. "What happened to Matt? Did you check for a pulse?"

"Yes. I think he's been dead for a while."

"Let me see." Rob eased her aside. "Damn, not Matt." He wiped a stray tear from Sissy's face. "I'm sorry, but you two need to wait in the other room. Officers, come here."

Sissy grabbed my hand and pulled me away from the office as Rob and the policemen crowded by the doorway. We sat in silence until she asked me why I was there. Before I started to explain, Rob came over, so I only had to tell my story once.

"I must seem like the nosiest person, but really I'm not," I said. "I should have just called the guys about the open door, but I didn't, and now..."

"It's all right, don't worry," Sissy said with such kindness in her eyes and voice that it made me tear up again. "I'm sorry it was you, but I'm glad a friend found him. Neal wouldn't have handled it this well, trust me."

"Poor Neal," Rob said as he finished writing in his notebook. "Those two were thick as thieves. I need to talk to the rest of the team that's showing up. Sit tight for a second."

Sissy held my hand as we waited. It was comforting to have her with me, but I couldn't shake the feeling I was bad luck. Was Ruby right that I invited trouble? I closed my eyes, trying to keep the tears from falling. I was being selfish when Matt's body lay in the next room. Why would anyone kill him? Everyone loved him.

Except Neal last night.

I opened my eyes to find Sissy staring at me. I smiled weakly. "Sorry, I can't stop thinking about Neal."

"I understand. He'll be devastated."

I nodded, but I must have given some hint that I didn't quite agree as she squeezed my hand and laughed softly. Not the response I expected.

"Have you seen Matt and Neal fight? They do that all the time, so don't worry."

"That's what Neal said last night."

"It won't make it easier for him, but they would argue like brothers. And trust me, I know what that's like."

"I bet you do." I smiled back at her, but I still worried that last night's fight wasn't just another argument.

Finally, Rob came over to us. "You both can go home now, but don't talk to anyone. I'll come over to the apartment building soon."

"Can you tell us anything?" Sissy pleaded.

"I can't say much yet, but it looks like a robbery turned homicide."

A robbery? The baseball bat worried me. It reminded me of the pipe standing in the bathroom's corner when I found Kelly. It was just a small detail, but it bothered me. And the murderer covered Matt's body like Kelly's, although differently, I had to admit.

"Sammy, are you ready to go?" Sissy's voice snapped me out of my thoughts. I was eager to get home but dreaded explaining to my friends about Matt's death. Unless someone there already knew.

39

"Good morning, beautiful ladies. Please tell me you have coffee. We're out. I'm hoping Matt is out getting some. Hey, what's going on?"

Neal stopped rambling as he sauntered along the balcony toward the stairs to the courtyard as we came in. With his rumpled hair, wrinkled T-shirt, and stained sweatpants, it looked like he just rolled out of bed.

Sitting at my outdoor table were William and Libby. Against Rob's instructions, Sissy called them as we walked home, so they already knew about Matt.

"I'm used to giving bad news, so I'll talk to Neal," Sissy said before rushing up the stairs. "Neal, come with me to your apartment."

"Why? What's going on? Sammy, did you find another body?" He laughed but stopped abruptly. "Wait, something happened, didn't it?"

Sissy whispered in his ear, and by his initial reaction of surprise and disbelief, it was obvious she told him about Matt. He collapsed against her and bawled. It was gut-wrenching to hear him cry, to see the happy-go-lucky party guy in such pain. How could I have considered him a murderer? He was an amazing actor if he was the killer.

I watched Sissy seamlessly guide Neal to his apartment. His sobbing turned to wailing as Sissy closed the door. I walked over to my landlords.

"Oh, honey," Libby said as she embraced me. William gave me a sympathetic smile as he reached for the keys in my outstretched hand. We moved inside, closing my door to Neal's sobs.

It was déjà vu as they led me into my apartment. William made coffee and added whiskey to all three cups without asking while Libby sat next to me on my love seat. No one spoke as we drank our coffee. I told them what happened since Sissy only gave them a bare-bones version of my story. Their faces revealed nothing; I didn't know if they thought I was lying or they were still in shock.

William spoke first. "It's a real shame. He was a good man, and he worked hard. And he and Neal were a solid team."

"They're like brothers," Libby said as she handed me a tissue while she took one for herself. "I remember when they quit their jobs to start the tour company. They were nervous, but I knew they would do well. My boys..."

William returned to the coffee maker to brew another pot. I hoped we had enough whiskey to get through the day. As he refilled my cup, we heard a knock at my door. William answered it to find Rob and his partner, Detective Gammon, standing outside.

"William, I didn't expect to find you here," Rob said.

"I told you Sissy called them already," Detective Gammon said as she entered the apartment after Rob. "Let me guess, Sissy is with Neal?"

"Yes, she had to tell him," Libby explained. "Neal came out, and we couldn't hide what happened."

Rob's face turned red, whether from embarrassment or anger, I wasn't sure. At the office, Rob said it looked like a robbery, but did they find something that implicated Neal?

Detective Gammon said, "You should never let Sissy leave a scene." I expected her to be angry, but she seemed a bit amused. "In any case, the word is already out, so I bet Neal has calls and texts about it."

The detective surprised me, but she understood how fast gossip traveled in the neighborhood. Hopefully this same information would help solve Matt's murder. I hoped it also meant she wasn't concerned that Neal was involved.

William closed the door behind them and went to my kitchen. Libby got up and joined him, so Detective Gammon took her place next to me while Rob stood across from us.

"Miss Richardson, this is unusual, you realize. I don't think I've had a witness find two bodies in such a short amount of time, if at all," Detective Gammon said as she stared at me. Again, she played the bad cop, but I understood. My actions were suspect, to say the least.

"It wasn't just a body she found; it was our Matt," Libby interrupted. "Don't you call him a body!" And with that she threw herself against William's chest.

"I'm sorry, Miss Libby, I didn't mean any disrespect. I understand Matt was well-liked here in the building and in the neighborhood," she said. The detective had a softer side.

"I'm sorry, too, Christine. We're all upset. Ask your questions. Is that all right, Sammy?" Libby said as she wiped her tears on my kitchen towel.

"Sure," I said, trying to sound confident. As hard as it was describing finding the woman a few days ago, it was easy compared to talking about Matt. I told my story without stopping until I described Matt's body. Libby and I both cried while Rob handed me a pack of tissues printed with the NOPD website and phone number.

"Why did you go in the office?" Detective Gammon asked as I finished wiping my tears. "Did you plan to meet with Matt that morning?"

"Sammy had nothing to do with this, so don't you dare accuse her!" Libby exploded. It felt good to have Libby defend me.

"We're not accusing her of anything. Sammy didn't have any blood on her, and Matt had passed a long time before she found him," Rob said.

"Yes, we'll know more later," Detective Gammon said. "The perpetrator emptied the cashbox, so it appears to be a robbery."

"But the laptop was still on the front desk," I said as I sat up a little straighter on the couch. "Wouldn't a robber take it? And why would a robber take the time to put the murder weapon in the corner of the room?"

The detectives looked at each other, and I realized I wasn't the only one who noticed those things. Rob said, "Thank you for your observations, Sammy. We need to talk to Neal now. Here's my card again if you remember anything else."

"You can ask Sissy to have him call you." Detective Gammon gave her first smile to me as we laughed a bit. A little levity helped, but it didn't last for long.

"Libby, I'll go with them. Sissy might need help," William said as he followed the detectives out.

"Yes, do that," Libby said as she shut the door behind him. Under her breath, she said, "I pray Neal had nothing to do with this."

It surprised me that she was worried about Neal and

that she would say it out loud. If he had something to do with it, I doubted Libby would forgive him.

40

Libby left not long after William but not before she insisted I eat a slice of toast and drink some water. I appreciated her mothering tactics, but it was a relief to have the apartment to myself. As I flopped on the couch, trying to decide if I should nap or shower, someone knocked on my door. I wished I could ignore it, but if it was Neal, I needed to see him.

Instead it was Joey. "Hey, the news is all around the Quarter. I can't believe it."

"Me neither." I ushered him in. As much as I preferred not to talk anymore about the murder, I didn't want to be ungrateful for Joey's thoughtfulness.

"Thanks." He sat at the kitchen counter while I made more coffee. "I'll miss Matt. He was a good friend."

I handed him a mug as I considered his statement. Were they close friends? Matt always seemed standoffish with him, but he was that way with Connor, too.

"Did the police say what happened?"

"They think it's a robbery. Have you heard anything around the neighborhood?"

"Not really. Have you talked to Neal yet?"

"No. Sissy broke the news to him."

"He's going to be hurting for a while, especially after that big fight they had last night. How are you holding up?"

There was a quick knock and then Sissy entered.

"You need to lock your door from now on! Oh, hi, Joey. You heard about Matt, I take it."

"Everyone's talking about it. I wanted to check in on Neal. Did he say what happened?"

"No, he knows nothing more than what the police and I told him. There better not be talk of Neal being involved. He loved Matt like a brother. We all did." Sissy's hard façade crumbled as she delivered those last words. She regained her composure. "Get the word out that Neal is a good man and didn't hurt Matt."

"Yes, ma'am, I'll do that. I'm sorry I didn't mean to imply anything. I like them both," Joe said as he put his cup on the counter. "Just tell Neal I'm around if he needs me."

"Bye, Joey," I called out to him as he closed the door behind him. I turned back to Sissy. "I think you scared him."

She sat down on the stool and shook off the coffee I offered. She nodded to the bottle of whiskey I raised, so I poured her a healthy shot.

"I didn't mean to, but I'm concerned about Neal. He was a mess after talking with Rob and Christine. He's finally resting after I gave him a sleeping pill."

"I'm worried, too. How's he going to get through this?"

"With the help of good friends like us," she replied as she chugged her drink.

"Agreed. Hey, Sissy, I need your help now."

"Anything. Unless you had something to do with this mess." Sissy's angry face made me glad I was innocent.

"Of course not! It's just that I'm afraid the police will suspect Neal, and I'm not sure he has an alibi."

"What do you mean?"

I relayed more details of last night's fight, particularly their anger and the fact that Joey and some random strangers witnessed it, too. I shared that Neal stayed at the bar when Joey, Connor, and I left around 11:30 p.m.

"So, he could have gone to the office," I said. "But then again, I guess Joey or Connor could have, too."

"Hold it. You said Connor walked you back."

And much to my embarrassment, I told her about looking for Connor after he walked me home only to watch him go out the front gate.

Sissy raised her eyebrows at my last statement. "I guessed you and Connor had a connection. Don't read anything into him leaving. I've seen him go to work at odd hours. And Joey seems like a decent guy. Do you think one of them had something to do with Matt's death?"

After she spoke, I realized I sounded crazy. It seemed outrageous that I could accuse our friends of murder. But the crime scene was wrong, and my gut told me that Kelly's and Matt's deaths were connected. Was I making more of a mess out of the situation?

"No, not really," I lied to her. "I'm just overwhelmed with all that's happened. I won't say anything to the police about the fight. I don't want to make it worse for Neal."

"If you'd like, I'll tell Rob about it, and he can decide if it's something to follow up on. Don't share your concerns with Libby. She wouldn't understand."

My door was getting a workout as someone else was knocking. Sissy answered it and was engulfed in a hug from Connor.

"Oh, Sissy, it's you. I mean, hi," he said. "I just talked to

Momma about Matt. Sammy, I'm so sorry this happened to you."

I walked over to him and let him pull me into his arms. Sissy smiled. "You're in good hands, well...arms, now, so I'll go."

Before she pulled the door closed, she stepped back in and looked at me. "Sammy, don't worry anymore. Rob will figure this out."

"Thanks, Sissy, for everything."

Connor sat down on my love seat and asked me to tell him what happened. When I finished, he reached for my hand. "You seem to have some bad luck. Matt was a good man. He was quiet, but I feel like he was always aware of what was going on."

I found that last statement to be interesting. Matt was observant, I agreed. Did Matt see something or discover the truth about the diary or Kelly or....

"Earth to Sammy! You look like you've got a lot on your mind. I'm sorry, but I have to leave. I need to check on Momma before I go back to the restaurant. She loved Matt like a son. He was a better son to her than me."

"Oh, I doubt that."

"No, it's true. Momma loves everyone like her own."

"She and your dad have been good to me," I said. "I'm thankful for their support with all these horrific situations."

"You've been involved in a bunch of strange stuff since you got here."

"Yes, and I wonder if it's all connected." I let that slip. I didn't want to go into it with him, but I said it anyway.

"You think so? Matt didn't know that girl, did he?"

"No one knew her." At least no one admitted it. "My suspicious mind is working overtime. Time to rest. And I'm sure Libby is eager to see you."

Before he left, I said, "Hey, Connor. Let me know if anyone in the neighborhood heard anything about Matt. Maybe someone saw him."

"I can ask around. Their office is away from the night action, but someone could have been out and about." And with that he kissed me on the cheek and closed the door behind him.

Out and about like you? I wanted to chase after him and question him, but I stopped myself. Did I want to know the answer? I'd rather not suspect him, or Neal or Joey. I crawled into bed, hoping a nap would clear my head and heart, even if only for a short time.

41

I napped longer than I expected. When I woke, I felt groggy, not refreshed as I had hoped. I swung out of bed and checked my phone. A voicemail was waiting from Detective Gammon, asking me to come to the station in the morning. Would Rob offer me a T-shirt again, or was there another prize for finding a second body?

As I walked to the kitchen to get a glass of water, the sounds from outside startled me. The screeching of metal furniture moving, and yelling made me open my door. Neal with a bottle of Jack Daniels in one hand and a chair in the other was the source of the noise.

"Neal, are you okay?"

"What do you think? My friend is dead," he yelled as he hurled the chair across the courtyard. It hit the brick wall with a bang. "It's all your fault!"

He collapsed in the remaining seat and swigged from his whiskey bottle. His puffy, red eyes bore into me; there was no doubt his grief was directed toward me.

"You found two bodies in one week, Sammy. That's not

friggin' normal. Are you a witch? Are you trouble like Ruby said?"

"I don't know why this happened, Neal. I'm so sorry," I said. I leaned against my doorframe, wishing I had the words to comfort him.

"Things were fine until you showed up. We're your friends and then you bring this all on us." Neal tried to stand up, but he fell back onto his chair. "And on top of it all, I heard you said I had something to do with it."

"Neal, no…"

"Oh, yeah. The rumor on the street is you suspect one of your buddies killed that girl. You think I did it and I murdered my best friend." He finished his bottle with a loud gulp. "I'm innocent."

"I know you didn't do it," I pleaded as I stepped back into my apartment. "You wouldn't hurt anyone, I'm sure."

I understood his anger, but I didn't want to be the brunt of it any longer. I feared his rage would turn physical, and I was no match for him, drunk or sober.

"Aren't we friends, Sammy?" He staggered up this time and stumbled. "Don't you trust me?"

"Neal, stop it."

I stepped warily out of my apartment, relieved to see Andrew striding straight to Neal. His commanding voice and presence calmed me. I hadn't realized I was holding my breath and clenching my hands until Andrew arrived.

Libby and William came over next and stopped by the main building. Libby held on to William, seemingly for support. William turned his wife toward the door and opened it. She looked back, turning from me to Neal. I could sense her disappointment as if Neal and I were misbehaving children. The scene must have shattered her *We're all one big, happy family* belief. And even though Neal was the one yelling, I thought I was the one she blamed.

"Oh, hey. I'm okay. Y'all don't need to worry about me," Neal shouted toward Libby before she closed the door. He let Andrew take the whiskey bottle from his hand and stood next to him. "I just wanted to talk to Sammy. It's all good. Right, Sammy?"

No, it wasn't all good, but I nodded my head.

"Andrew, you get what it's like to lose someone. I mean it's different because Matt and I were just friends. But it sucks losing someone you love."

"Yes, Neal, I understand. Let's take you up to your bed. You need a good night's sleep."

Andrew guided the wobbly Neal upstairs and into his apartment. Before he closed the door, Andrew looked over the balcony and said, "Samantha, go rest, too. I'll take care of him."

"Please don't take Neal's outburst to heart. We're a family," William said as he walked over to me. He put his arm around me and escorted me to my door. "You know how it is. Families fight and then they make up."

No, I didn't know. My family didn't argue. We rarely disagreed, and if we did, we kept it to ourselves. This level of confrontation frightened me.

"Give him time. Libby and I will keep tabs on him and he'll come around," he said as he kissed me on top of my head, to my surprise. "Don't worry too much."

At least he told me not to worry too much, because I would worry. I liked Neal and now he hated me. I was a horrible person to imagine he or even Joey or Connor could commit murder.

I locked my door and went straight back to bed after

taking two sleeping pills. I hoped it would help me sleep, because my mind raced with thoughts of doubt and guilt and sadness. New Orleans was not turning out to be the future I wanted it to be.

185

42

I woke up the next day in a daze. The medicine helped me fall asleep, but I stirred every hour. Any sound outside made me flinch, but I stayed in bed all night. The thought of finding something or someone in front of my apartment terrified me.

I assumed the early morning noise I heard had been Andrew. I found a note tucked halfway under my front door.

Samantha,

Please don't fret over yesterday's disturbance. Neal is not himself. Come to my shop this afternoon.

Yours Truly,

Andrew

At least he wasn't angry at me. A text from Sissy made me add her to the list. *Don't worry about Neal. I didn't tell him what you said. Everything will be OK.*

I hoped she was right. My mood picked up until I walked by Libby's café on my way to the police station. I might have been wrong, but I swear she turned her head as she saw me in the café's doorway. I lost my desire for food, so I left before I found out how she was feeling about me.

Detective Gammon didn't offer me coffee, but our meeting was cordial and quick. Rob didn't bring up the concerns I shared with Sissy about the guys, so either he preferred not to ask in front of his partner or he believed I was crazy.

Rob walked me out like last time and once again offered a T-shirt. I declined, and he laughed, "I guess I should offer you a badge instead. Sissy told me of your worries about Neal, Connor, and Joey. I also know you spoke to Kelly's roommates at the bar."

"Oh, yes, I..." I stammered.

"Don't worry," he said as he opened the door and walked outside with me. "I understand you're concerned about your friends, but we'll check into it. And I'm sure your visit to Kelly's workplace was to offer sympathy and not investigate."

"Of course," I lied. This was becoming a bad habit.

"Do you need to tell me anything else?"

"No." The key necklace hiding underneath my shirt was an albatross, but I wasn't ready to turn it over to the police.

"Good." He shook my hand. "Again, I'm sorry this happened to you. Take care, Miss Sammy."

Guilt weighed heavily on me as I left, but not enough to make me go back. If the investigation into Kelly's death stalled, I promised myself I would bring the key over to them. Hopefully Andrew discovered what the key opened, and that's why he asked me to his shop this afternoon.

It wasn't even 10:30 a.m., so I had time to kill. Not a phrase I should use anymore.

My growling stomach suggested I visit the French Market, a combination of a food market and flea market in one section and permanent stores in the other. Café du Monde's beignets and café au lait tempted me, as did Aunt

Sally's pralines, but I kept walking until I reached the grocery side. I would find fruits and vegetables there, and my body needed healthy food after yesterday's diet of coffee and whiskey.

I bought the makings for a salad and added a few apples to my shopping bag. I avoided the alligator samples and the booths offering Bloody Mary's topped with a variety of fried foods. I chose a berry smoothie that proclaimed it would cure any ailment. If it fixed my increasing anxiety and sadness, I would drink one every day.

Just like the grocery side sold healthy and unhealthy food, this flea market was also contradictory. From hand-crafted items such as paintings and knitwear to mass-produced products like suitcases and sunglasses, the market stood as a strange representation of the city. Like New Orleans, the French Market offered objects that were new and old, beautiful and tacky, and from the past and present.

As I passed yet another table piled high with tourist T-shirts, I stopped dead in my tracks. BB dolls filled a small square table, their hand-stitched faces smiling at me.

"Hi. Let me know if you have any questions. Are you familiar with BB dolls?" asked a young woman with an engaging smile wearing a "BB Dolls Are Back" button on her sequin-covered T-shirt under a pair of faded overalls.

"Yes, I am. I have one, well, two, well, three, well, one," I said. I only had one now since the second doll was in police custody, along with the doll left with Kelly's body. She must have assumed I indulged in a fried alligator-topped Bloody Mary with all this stuttering.

Working at a tourist location I guess she was used to it as she ignored my babbling and kept talking: "That's great! I'm Stacy. My grandmother created them. I'm carrying on the line. I have pictures of the original set of dolls. Would you like to see them?"

She pulled out a photo album and flipped through the pages. "Grammy started off with ten different dolls about thirty years ago. She sold them here at the market. Do you see yours in here?" She turned the page to show me photos of each one.

"That's mine. She has that dress, and the hair is the same."

Stacy looked closer at the picture. "That was Grammy's favorite. She based it on my mother's favorite dress and her name, Sarah."

"Sarah?"

"Yes, that's my momma's name. I made about six of those dolls like her after I cleaned out my grandmother's house a few months back. They sold quickly."

"Do you remember who bought them?"

She shook her head. "Sorry, no. I'm not good with faces with so many people coming through here. Why do you ask?"

"Oh, just wondering which friend purchased my other dolls," I said as my head throbbed.

Someone knew me from my childhood. Who else would have bought me a replica doll and left it for me? The doll at the murder scene was not there by chance. Three BB dolls were now part of my life, my story.

"Wow, you must be reminiscing something fierce there," Stacy said as I broke free of my thoughts. "Is your name Sarah? Or do you just like pink dresses?"

Was I Sarah? "No, I'm Samantha, but I like pink dresses."

She smiled and produced a doll wearing a pink sundress. "Perhaps this would be a great addition to your collection?"

Instead, I picked out one wearing purple overalls with the BB logo on the back pocket. "My friend's daughter will love this one. I like the updated style."

After the information I learned, I felt obligated to make a purchase. She wrapped it up in a gift bag just like the one my duplicate doll arrived in on my front step. "Here you go! Thanks! I hope she enjoys it."

I thanked her and left the French Market and headed to Jackson Square to sit on a bench and try to wrap my head around this new information. I took out my notebook again and looked at my notes the other day. I added these:

Doll = Sarah
Body = Sarah
Me = Sarah?

Was I Sarah? Could I have been saying "Sarah" instead of "Sam" when they found me after the hurricane? Two-year-olds weren't known for their stellar pronunciation.

The brass band outside the park ended their song with a loud bang, which made me jump and drop my notebook and pen on the ground. As I bent over to pick them up, I noticed a man out of the corner of my eye. A baseball hat shielded his face, so he was unrecognizable as he hustled toward the Decatur Street exit. Perhaps my paranoia was acting up again, but I was positive he had been watching me. And he looked familiar. Frank, Connor, Joey, and Neal were similar in build so it could have been any of them. Or Andrew, but I couldn't imagine him wearing a baseball hat.

I would know if it was Andrew by going to his store. Sitting on the bench wasn't doing me any good, just making me jumpy. I hoped he had information about my key. And I needed a friend.

43

———————

As I walked to Andrew's shop, I kept an eye out for the man from Jackson Square, but I didn't see him. From the stacks of boxes piled throughout the store, it wasn't Andrew in the park.

"Samantha, darling! Come in! By chance, can you help your poor old friend out?" Andrew asked me from behind a stack of half-opened boxes. "I'm overwhelmed today."

"I'm happy to help. Would you like me to open more boxes or put away the new books?"

"Thank goodness," he said as he handed me his box cutter. "I need to check these off the packing lists and figure out where to place them. They weren't scheduled to arrive until next week. On top of that I was late to the store this morning."

"Oh. Were you with Neal?" I lowered my head to hide my watering eyes.

He stepped around the boxes and lifted my chin. "Samantha, please don't let last night weigh on you too heavily, although I know that's easier said than done," he said. "I stayed at his apartment until Sissy relieved me.

191

She'll get him through his hangover and help him begin the healing process."

"I'm glad to hear he's not alone."

"But you're feeling alone, aren't you?"

"Yes, but I also feel like all this is my fault. Everything was fine in the building before I came."

Andrew's laughter startled me. "Oh, my dear, you have no idea where you moved into! Thibodeaux Mansion is no Peyton Place. Wait, you're too young for that reference. What I mean is, there have always been problems or issues with our neighbors."

I sat down on an unopened box and tried to absorb what he was saying. His honesty was the kick in the butt I needed, but I wasn't expecting it. He pulled up a box and sat next to me.

"Now, I won't gossip about our friends, as it's their responsibility to share their stories with you," he said as he patted my hand. "But I will tell you that everybody has their own troubles, even yours truly. You'll get through this just like everyone else in New Orleans."

I stood up, wiped the tears that had snuck down my face, and put my hands on my hips. "You're right, I'll get through this. If I can survive a hurricane as a toddler, I will make it through whatever this is that I'm in the middle of. But right now, let's get through your boxes."

For the next two hours, we unpacked all the boxes and shelved the books. It would have taken less time, but customers came into the store in waves. Each sale was a history lesson of New Orleans. Andrew's success was obvious; his passion for books and for placing them with the right person made him and his shop special.

"Now, sit down while I get us some lemon water and give you your books," he said as we emptied the last box. He steered me toward the sitting area. "I haven't had the chance to go through them as I planned before you arrived, but reading them on your own might be a good distraction."

Andrew put our drinks on coasters on the table along with two books. The first was *The New Orleans Guide to Cemeteries*. It was full of glossy photos of the cemeteries in the city. It included maps and detailed history on each place. I couldn't think of any other city that had books and tours dedicated to its graveyards.

The other book, *New Orleans Advertisements and More* was softbound and thinner and displayed black-and-white and color pictures of everything from houses, mausoleums, housewares, and clothing. It was like a catalog of products made or sold in New Orleans from the 1800s to the 1980s.

"I emailed the photo of the key to my friend Remmy, but he's swamped with researching his latest book about Marie Laveau. He told me he thought the key was from the 1800s, but what it opens, he doesn't know yet. He sent over his advertisement book so you can see if your key is in there."

"That was very kind of him. Let me know what I owe him. Is the other book his, too?"

"You owe nothing. Remmy owes me ten times over in the books I've given him for his research. And the cemetery book is mine."

"A. B. Dumas is you?"

"My pen name," he said with just the slightest hint of a smile. "I wrote that during my teaching years. I tried to keep my professional and writing lives separate back then. Now they're one and the same. A pseudonym makes me mysterious, don't you think?"

I laughed along with him and then said, "Everyone is mysterious in New Orleans. Except me."

"My dear, you are beautiful and interesting and kind,

and those are much better qualities to have." He squeezed my hand and took a sip of his water. "Now, let me know if you find anything in the books. I'm not sure if my book will be of help, but if nothing else, I wanted you to see that death is just a part of the New Orleans' culture."

"There's no doubt about that," I agreed. "I prefer to learn about historic deaths, not current ones, though."

"That's understandable. Perhaps these books will distract you from the present."

"Thanks, Andrew. I appreciate your help." I picked up my bags from the market and added the books to them. "Call me if you need me in the store again."

I kissed him on the cheek and headed back down Royal Street to my apartment. While I still had the events of the last few days on my mind, my heart was lighter after an afternoon with Andrew. The lightness fell to darkness as I entered the courtyard to my least favorite neighbor covered head to toe in white chiffon, chanting and waving a smoking bundle of sticks.

44

"Trouble be gone. You are not welcome here. Only good, only light may cross my threshold. Goddess of Good, protect me and my loved ones from all negative forces."

"Amen?" I asked as I walked toward my door, trying to place the overpowering scent wafting through the courtyard. It reminded me of the smell that would leak from the dorm rooms during my freshman year, but I couldn't imagine Ruby smoking pot outside, if at all.

"Don't mock what you don't understand," she answered with a frown and then thrust her burning sticks at me. "I am cleansing this area for my safety. You should thank me."

"What exactly am I thanking you for?"

"You are clueless about the spiritual world," she said. "I am smudging to remove the negative spirits and bring purity back. You attract bad spirits."

"Yes, I recall you said I was trouble."

Cleopatra and Nefertiti sauntered over from the garden and jumped up on the table. Their owner didn't like me, but they appeared to from their constant purring as I stroked their heads. Their soft fur and gentle meows soothed me, unlike Ruby.

"Yes, you seem to be a magnet for negativity," she said as she motioned for her cats to come to her, but they wouldn't move. I really liked these cats.

"You found a dead woman the other day. And then you discovered poor Matthew..." She whispered Matt's name as she blinked rapidly, I assumed to keep back tears. Did Ruby have some humanity left in that hard shell? Just as I was about to give her the benefit of the doubt, she ruined it.

"I suggest you cleanse your home and your heart. Take the sage and instructions. You need help." She placed an unlit bundle of sticks and an index card on my table. She grabbed her wriggling cats and stomped to her apartment. "Open your mind and heart, if not for your sake, do it for those who share your physical space. Maybe Matthew would still be alive if you had."

Shocked by her words and the slam of her door, I sat in my chair as my tears streamed down my face. I didn't need Ruby to make me feel guilty; I was doing a good job on my own. I understood she lashed out because of her own grief, but it still bothered me more than it should have.

I swallowed one last sob and gathered my belongings and the sage and the card from Ruby. Tempting as it was to leave it outside, the herb might be poisonous to animals. Since Cleopatra and Nefertiti were my only friends, I didn't want to hurt them.

"Drama queen," I said out loud as I flopped on my love seat. I had friends of the humankind, but if something else happened, I wasn't so sure.

I curled up in a ball and squeezed my eyes tight as if I could protect myself from my reality. It didn't work; the image of Matt's battered face filled my head no matter how hard I tried to banish it. I pulled myself up from the couch, wiped my tears, and let out my last sob.

I picked up Ruby's cleansing materials to throw them in the trash, but the handwriting on the instructions caught my eye. I assumed it was a standard manual given with the sage bundle, but I was wrong. Written in an elegant cursive, she had addressed the index card to me and explained the steps to follow, including a short prayer to recite. On the back of it she wrote, *May the Goddess of Good protect you.*

Confusion and anger fought with hope and peace in my head. How could she give me a spiritual gift while berating me? Life with Ruby was filled with contradictory words and actions. I didn't know what to make of this last interaction, but decided to be open-minded and try her personalized ritual.

Like lighting the candles at St. Louis Cathedral, I wasn't confident I was performing it correctly, but I followed each of Ruby's steps. After smudging every room, including my bathroom, I stood in the center of my apartment, waiting for the purity and peace Ruby's card said I would receive after the ceremony. The only result was a cough from the burning sage.

Nothing was working, so I headed to bed. I didn't bother to put on my pajamas or brush my teeth; I crawled under my covers and hoped sleep would take me away from this world for a night.

45

The following three days were the longest of my life. I hid from the world in my apartment, not able to face anyone or anything. I alternated between drinking coffee and wine and sleeping on my bed or love seat. One minute I would make lists of things to do in New Orleans and then I would rip them up. Next, I was online looking at plane fares and rentals in San Francisco. Then I would just collapse on my couch and sigh and repeat the cycle.

My phone kept me connected to the outside world. Sissy texted that she was working for three days but call her if I needed her. Andrew left a voicemail each day, imploring me to visit him at the shop, but I texted him that I was sick. I gave the same reply to Libby, William, Connor, and Joey's texts.

I knew I should have talked to them, but I was still hurt from Neal's outburst. With my confusion about whether I should stay or go, I didn't want to deal with anyone.

On the night of day three, I finally opened the door to nonstop knocking. The sight of me in my dirty pajamas, greasy hair, and a glass of wine in my hand should have scared him off, but Connor stood his ground.

"Hi. What do you want?" He was the last person I wanted to see, and I couldn't keep the irritation out of my voice.

"I'm worried about you. You can't hide forever. Can I come in?"

I flung the door open and stomped over to my love seat. Whatever chance I had with him was long gone, so I didn't care about what I said or did.

To my surprise, he sat next to me and took the glass out of my hand. I tried to avoid his eyes, but he wouldn't let me. He kept following my gaze until I stopped moving and stared back at him.

"Sammy, we're all worried. Yes, all of us," he said in response to my shaking head. "I mean it. We're in our own world these days. Losing Matt hit us hard. But don't let this keep you from us. We're good people. Honest."

I didn't want to agree, but I nodded. Damn, he was being nice, and I was a disaster.

"Okay, let's put you back together. Go shower. Yes, shower while I clean up a bit. No offense, but you and this place stink."

He pulled me off the love seat and pushed me toward the bathroom. He was ever the gentlemen and closed the door behind him. In my state, I couldn't invite him to join me, although that thought made for a much better shower.

I washed up and put on the only pair of matching pajamas I owned. The flowered print and modest design of the set wasn't sexy, but I knew nothing would happen with Connor that night, if ever.

I opened the bathroom door to find him putting clean

sheets on my bed. There wasn't a sexier sight than Connor making my bed. If he got in it, that would have been perfect.

"Hey, you look great. Feel better?" He came around the bed and gave me a hug. I tried not to melt in his arms, but the loneliness of the past few days was too much. "You will be okay. We'll get through this. I promise."

I got into my bed, and he pulled the duvet up to my chin and brushed my hair from my forehead. A gentle kiss on my lips lingered for a moment, but then he withdrew with a soothing smile.

"Everything's going to be okay," he said.

I rested my head on my pillow after thanking him for taking care of me. I wish I believed him, but with all that had happened would everyone forgive me or not blame me?

"Go to sleep; everything will be better in the morning."

And with that the door clicked shut as I drifted to sleep with dreams that tomorrow would be a better day.

46

Waking up to a clean house was a good way to start my day. I tried to think positively like Connor suggested the night before. I needed to decide on my future whether it meant staying here or moving somewhere else. Where would I go? With all the drama of the past few weeks, I still considered New Orleans to be my home.

The beeps on my phone alerted me to a slew of texts. Connor's was the first, and I responded with a thanks and that I felt better. The next were from Libby and William. Libby's was a short but sweet *Scones are outside your door. I hope you're OK.* William's text was, *We hope you are fine. Life will be back to normal soon.*

My face hurt and I realized I was smiling. I hadn't used those muscles for the past few days. I grabbed the blueberry scones from my doorstep and made coffee. As I sat at my kitchen counter, I opened my notebook and my copy of the diary. Someone left it and the key for me to find. At first it appeared to be a scavenger hunt written in a diary form, but where did the key lead?

I could have brushed off the diary and key as a coincidence, but when I added the BB dolls at my front door and then on a body, I couldn't. It had to be tied together. What was the point of all of this? There had to be a point. I reviewed the places the journal took me to again, but it was just a list to me. What were they meant to tell me?

I snatched my original BB doll off the shelf and stared at her. She was the Sarah doll, but did that mean anything? I kept turning her over and running my fingers over her as if she held a secret that I had missed over the years. I grabbed a pair of scissors to cut her open when there was a knock on the door.

"Hey, don't attack! Just checking in on you!" Joey stood wide-eyed on my doorstep with a box in his hands.

"What? Oh, the scissors! Sorry, I was working on a project. Come in."

"Are you sure? I understand if you're on the defensive after everything that's gone on."

"Yes, come on in. I just have a lot on my mind." I put the scissors and doll away and closed the diary and my notebook.

"I bet. I haven't seen you out for a bit. And I brought you this."

"Aunt Sally's pralines! Wow, I love these. That was very thoughtful of you, Joey." I ripped open the box and unwrapped one of my favorite candies. Sugar, milk, butter, and pecans, or some variation of those ingredients, combined to make a flat, circular-shaped candy. They were sweet and melted in your mouth except for the slight crunch of the pecans.

He took a praline and said, "They're my favorite. I always feel better when I eat one."

"Me, too."

"What are you doing with the stuff on the counter? What's with the doll?"

"Oh, I'm just trying to sort things out."

"Seems like you've had a lot happen since you moved here."

"That's an understatement. Between the murders and the diary, I don't understand what's going on."

He raised his eyebrows as he sipped his coffee. "You think it's all tied together? What would that diary have to do with it?"

"I don't know," I said. "Nothing to do with Matt, I guess. I still didn't understand why that poor woman was killed in that house that the journal led me to."

"Sounds like you think it's about you, then."

"I know I must sound crazy. I just moved to New Orleans for a change, but it's become more than I expected."

"Change is a good thing," Joey said as he finally accepted a second praline. "But didn't you move here to find out about your past, too? You told us about it at the party that night. Any luck with it?"

"I did, but with everything that's happened, I'm going to forget about my birth family for a bit," I lied. "Too much is going on, and I need to focus on my future, my friends."

It was a half lie since I planned to keep investigating my past, but I was too exhausted to talk about it for the time being.

"I get it." Joey smiled. "Everyone here seems like family."

"Except Ruby."

"Oh no, Ruby's that eccentric relative everyone has. In other parts of the country, you hide her, but here in the South, we put her on the porch with a sweet tea and let her talk."

We laughed until there was a knock at the door.

"That's my cue to leave. If you want to talk about anything, I'm here for you."

I gave him a quick hug; maybe life was improving. The person knocked again, so I swung open the door to find Sissy standing there with a bottle of wine, two plastic cups that said, *Wine Not?* and a handful of purple bead necklaces.

"It's been a horrible week, and it's time we change it," Sissy said and put three necklaces around my neck. They covered up my key necklace that I wore by habit. After the past few days I considered throwing it in the Mississippi River.

"Oh, hey, Joey. Checking on our girl?" Sissy smiled at him and gave him a peck on the cheek before he walked out the door. She raised her eyebrows at me and smirked. I shook my head at her and mouthed, "Shut up."

"Yes, just brought her some candy. Pralines are good for everything," he said. "I meant what I said, Sammy. I'm here if you need me."

"Thanks, Joey. See you soon," I yelled as he strolled toward the front gate.

I turned my attention to Sissy. "What in the world are you holding, Sissy?"

"These are the essentials for the Mardi Gras parade we're going to this afternoon. It's a walking parade by the Krewe of Cork, and it's wine themed. We need our cups and a few necklaces to start out. By the end you'll have more beads and definitely more wine."

"It seems wrong to go out, Sissy. Everything seems wrong."

"I understand, but Matt loved New Orleans. Here we celebrate death so he would want us to go."

"I'm sure you're right, but I'm not up for it."

"I have a friend who thinks you should go. Wait here."

I expected to see Connor or Andrew, but my mouth dropped at the man Sissy brought out. His sad eyes met mine, but he gave a slight smile as he greeted me, "Hey, Sammy."

"Hey, Neal."

"Listen, I'm sorry about yelling at you the other day," he mumbled, so I stepped closer to hear him. "I know it's not your fault. I needed someone to blame, but I shouldn't have blamed you."

I wanted to be angry with him, but I couldn't. His pale face, red-ringed eyes, and slouched posture showed me he was still in pain. I bit my lip so as not to cry. "I'm so sorry. It seems like I brought this on you and everyone here."

Neal pulled me toward him, and we held each other. I don't know who needed the hug more, but I needed his absolution since I wasn't sure I would ever give it to myself.

We ended our embrace to find Sissy wiping tears from her face.

"Tough Sissy can cry sometimes, huh?" Neal smiled as he hugged her next.

"Oh, stop it. I'm only tough when I'm a nurse," she said and then playfully swatted Neal's arm. "I think we all feel better now. So, Sammy, Neal said he has work to do, but you and I are going to the parade. Matt loved this one, so we'll go in his honor."

"You two should represent the building, our family," Neal said as he held me tightly one more time. "I have to call Matt's parents about his memorial service, but don't worry. I'll be fine, I promise."

"I'll see you later, then?" I called out as he walked toward the stairs to his apartment.

"You bet. Have fun, ladies."

And with that I agreed to go with Sissy that afternoon. Hopefully, my life was on the mend here in New Orleans. Nothing else could go wrong, could it? I prayed the answer was no as I went inside to get ready for my first Mardi Gras parade.

47

"Follow the grapes," Sissy instructed as we came upon the crowds waiting for the parade to begin.

A man covered in purple balloons led the way for us as we tried to find an empty spot to view the procession. In between a gaggle of male Marilyn Monroes and a six-pack of life-sized wine bottles, we found our place.

I spotted Connor on the opposite sidewalk. He waved and shouted, "Going to work. Have fun, ladies!"

At least I think it was to us; the Marilyn Monroes were also calling to him. They sighed as he walked out of sight.

"That man attracts everyone's attention, doesn't he?" Sissy said. "I know he's got yours."

My cheeks felt warm, and I couldn't just blame it on the wine. "Connor is charming, but I don't need any more drama right now."

"I disagree. That's the kind of drama you want!"

The group of bottles noticed us giggling, and they offered us drinks from one of the many magnums they were carting around. I forgot Connor as the life-sized bottle of

Chardonnay poured more into my to-go cup. I worried about spilling it on the costumed people surrounding us. Those making their way down the street and the latecomers trying to find a space to stand jostled me constantly. I became numb to it, or it could have been the alcohol.

Mardi Gras in New Orleans reminded me of Halloween. From people dressed in full costumes like our new friends to those just wearing beads, everybody was part of the celebration. From what I gathered, it didn't matter if you weren't in the krewe; they expected everyone to participate.

I was thankful to have Sissy as my guide. This parade differed from what I learned at the museum since this was a walking parade. There would be no floats, just the krewe members strolling the route throwing trinkets at the crowds.

"Now, remember to shout and wave; otherwise, you'll come home empty-handed," she explained. "Yes, I'm serious. Don't give me that look."

"Aren't we too old to yell? I thought only the kids yelled."

"You're never too old, but you can be too sober. Drink up!"

I took a big sip and asked, "How's this? Throw me something, mister!" I waved my arms in the air like one of those inflatable waving tube men at car dealerships.

Sissy choked back her wine. "Honey, you're a natural!"

Between the laughter and the onslaught of beads, plastic cups, and decorated corks, I forgot about the past week and threw myself into the parade experience. I hadn't expected to love yelling and calling attention to myself, but it was addicting trying to get trinkets thrown to me.

A green-haired court jester stopped in front of me and draped a gold-beaded necklace with a wineglass ornament around my neck. I laughed and thanked him as he made his way back into the parade. In my giddiness, I tried to return to my spot and bumped into the people behind me.

"Sorry! Too many beads and wine, I guess," I said. I turned to see how much Sissy had collected, but she was missing. I couldn't imagine her leaving me here, so I scanned the area and discovered her standing in front of an art gallery. From her pursed lips and creased forehead, she appeared to be giving Rob and Detective Gammon a hard time.

"Sorry, again," I said as I pushed through the crowds to reach them. Most ignored me, but I annoyed the serious bead collectors as I disrupted their quest. I reached the back of the crowd and over to them.

"Hey, I didn't mean to leave you, but I saw them and had to talk to them. Now, you two tell her what you told me," Sissy commanded to an apparently irritated Detective Gammon and an embarrassed Rob.

"Hi, Miss Sammy. As I explained to Sissy, all we know is that both the woman you discovered and Matt were killed in a similar fashion, but we can't say it was the same assailant—"

"What about the hairs?" Sissy interrupted Rob.

"I'm getting to that." He gritted his teeth and spoke again: "We found brown hairs on both bodies, but not anything we can test for DNA."

"Many people have brown hair, so it's probably a coincidence," Detective Gammon interjected this time. "Besides you, Miss Richardson, there really isn't a connection between these murders. Before you say anything, Sissy, I'm not accusing your friend. I'm just saying there is no reason to connect the crimes. We've had several burglaries in the Quarter and we're exploring that theory regarding Matt's homicide."

Rob nodded his head in agreement as Sissy and I stared at them. It was comforting to have her there standing by me physically and emotionally. And from her death stare at her boyfriend, I knew she was on my side.

Detective Gammon broke the silence. "I can see you don't agree with us, but that's where we're at right now. I'm sure Rob will keep you posted. And, Miss Richardson, please call if you remember any details, big or small."

"I understand. Thanks for the information."

Sissy turned her cheek up for Rob to kiss her goodbye. He gave my arm a quick squeeze and whispered, "I'll let you know if something turns up. Be careful in the meantime, you hear?" He caught up to his partner declining a cup of wine from the group of tipsy grapes.

The update, or lack thereof, I should say, put a damper on my mood. I tried to yell for beads as the king and queen passed us by, but I'd lost the energy and interest. How could they think nothing connected the murders? The thread that linked them was thin, but Matt's death wasn't random. The way the bat was propped up was just like the pipe at Kelly's murder. And now there were hairs, and yes, I understood that that many people had brown hair. Including Neal, Connor, and Joey. Even William and Frank did, too. Great. I might as well accuse everyone in the neighborhood.

"Sammy!" Sissy yelled to get my attention as the parade goers left us. "Let's grab some dinner and some better drinks. This last batch of wine was awful."

"Sorry, I was daydreaming," I replied as I looked down at the dregs of some tasteless wine in my cup. "I agree. It's not rude to pour this out, is it?"

"Preferably in the trash, but it's not against parade rules to leave a drink unfinished. Let's get some food from Frankie's and better wine. She's been asking about you."

I emptied my cup in the nearest trash can and also tried to dump my bad mood. This wasn't the time to play detective, no matter how much my head told me I needed to find the answers to the murders.

48

———

We made our way to the store where Frankie was outside sweeping by the front door. "Hello, my darlings! Sammy, I've been so worried!" She squeezed me like an anaconda . I wasn't sure I could breathe much longer when a voice interrupted her death grip.

"Nonna, let her go now. She's been through enough, hasn't she?" Frank said as he pulled his grandmother away from me. "How are you, Miss Sammy? I'm sorry you found another body. We all liked Matt."

I gave an appreciative smile to him. "It's been tough. I never got to thank you properly for helping me that day."

"I'm glad I was there for you," he replied as he hugged me almost as tightly as Frankie. "Mr. Gregory has been asking about you. I can take you to visit him when you're ready."

"Did he get his bat back? If not, I want to buy him a new one."

"He hasn't, but he doesn't need it. He's organized a

neighborhood watch group. A whistle and a notebook are now his weapons against crime."

At least something good came out of that situation. "Thanks again for helping me. Thank goodness you were on that street at the right time."

"Glad to help a friend. I'm sorry you had that experience. I'll never forget that girl's face."

"Me, neither. Did you recognize her?"

"I might have seen her in the neighborhood, but I didn't know her," Frank said as he turned his back and continued washing the windows of the shop. "I heard you knew her."

"Really? She was a friend? Oh, my dear, two friends dead?" Frankie cried as she pulled me into another embrace.

"No, I didn't know her. I just saw her the night before. Strange coincidence, I guess," I said once Frankie let me go.

"A weird coincidence, for sure," Frank said. "Did a robber kill Matt? There have been some break-ins close to their office. We added a second security camera." He pointed to a shiny new outdoor camera directed at the front door.

"It makes me sad," Frankie said as she ushered us into the store. "Let's not talk of death, but of food. What do you ladies need for dinner?"

And with that we picked out lasagna and crawfish étouf-fée. Sissy insisted I select the wine since I was from California. I had to admit that I didn't know much about wine despite many trips to Napa Valley. The laughter that came from my friends made me forget my embarrassment and join them.

"That was real casual asking Frank if he knew the woman you found," Sissy said when we were a block away from the store. "You don't think he had anything to do with it, do you?"

"No, I can't imagine. He's okay, but he has brown hair, and it is strange that he was there at the right time. I'm such a horrible person to even consider him a suspect."

"Don't be too hard on yourself. You've had a lot happen to you." Sissy put her arm around me. "Let's forget about the mysteries for now and eat and drink."

We set up our meal at the table in the back of the courtyard. As we opened up the bottle of wine, a voice interrupted the stillness of the evening.

"There are my two favorite girls! Is there room for two old folks?" To my surprise, Libby, followed by William, headed toward us.

"I don't see any old folks, but y'all are welcome to join us," Sissy said. I took more cups out from the grocery bag. It was as if Frankie knew it would be more than just Sissy and I sharing the bottle.

"We're so happy to see you, Sammy," William said as he accepted a cup of wine from me and kissed me on the cheek.

"I'm glad to be out. It's all thanks to Sissy for taking me to my first parade."

"By the looks of it, you did well getting beads." Libby grinned as she pointed at all the necklaces covering my chest. "Sissy is the master at teaching newcomers how to yell for beads and trinkets. Wait until you go to the Muses parade and scream for a shoe."

"My head still hurts where the stiletto hit me." William rubbed his head.

"It's my favorite Mardi Gras souvenir," Libby said as she kissed the top of his head.

The evening continued with stories of previous parades.

We laughed until we cried about the tales that included one of Connor as a boy, trying to climb a float to get more beads, and Sissy, Matt, and Neal all dressing up as Princess Leia for the Chewbacchus parade. There was a story of Andrew, politely, but firmly, ushering a drunk Red Queen from Alice in Wonderland out of the courtyard as she shouted, "Off with his head!"

And even though I wasn't part of the stories, I enjoyed listening to them. How could I leave a place like this? This Mardi Gras season wouldn't be the best one for me, but today's parade was a good start to finding joy again in this city. As we performed a final toast to Matt and finished the wine, I made my mind up. I was staying in New Orleans.

49

"Thanks, again, Sissy! Yes, I'll be ready for this weekend's parades. I'll practice my *Throw me something, mister* moves," I said as we cleaned up the courtyard. William and Libby had left to meet friends at a party in the Garden District.

"You'd better! I'm heading over to Rob's place, but I'll be here in the morning, and I expect you to show me some fancy moves!" Sissy cackled as she headed upstairs.

While Matt's death still lingered in the air and in our hearts, it seemed we had made a step toward healing. Or maybe it was just me. Libby didn't seem disappointed with me as she hugged me at the end of the evening. And I felt much better when William leaned down to kiss me good-bye, and he whispered, "I told you, families work things out."

I locked my door, placed my wine cup on the coffee table, and flopped on the love seat to the sound of clinking beads. As I took them off, my cell phone rang.

"Hey, Madeline! I was thinking of you and Athena. I have more Mardi Gras beads than I can handle."

"I'm so jealous! Tell me all about it," my San Francisco best friend demanded.

I put my phone on speaker mode and babbled about the parade while removing all the bead necklaces. I kept my key necklace on out of habit. Remembering that I had even more souvenirs in my jacket pockets, I stood up and unloaded corks, plastic coins, and grape-shaped erasers. I grabbed a vase from the kitchen to showcase my trinkets.

"That sounds amazing! How's everything else going?"

Before I answered, I found a folded piece of paper. I assumed it would be an advertisement to a Bourbon Street bar or an invitation to a church service. Even with all the wine I drank, I remembered that Mardi Gras was the celebration before Lent.

As I opened the paper, I knew at once it wasn't an ad for sinning or repenting. It wasn't a bar selling two-for-one drinks. It wasn't a church trying to save my soul.

It was a murderer offering me one last clue in the deadly diary scavenger hunt.

50

"Samantha? Hey, are you still there?"

"Yes, sorry. I found something strange in my pocket."

How did this end up with all the other stuff I got? I closed my eyes and tried to relive the day, but so much had happened. I bumped into so many people before, during, and after the parade that anyone could have slipped the paper in my hands or pocket. Did Connor follow us after we saw him? Joey or even Neal might have been there. Frank could have put it in my coat at the store.

"What did you find?"

"It's another entry to that diary," I said and then explained the whole story including Matt's murder.

"I'm so sorry about your friend. Read the paper to me."

I paced my living room and read out loud:

Last Entry

It's til death do us part for me and my love. Death for me that is. It's not my fault, and it's not his fault. It's her fault. She ruined everything.

Before my love put me in this new world here's the clue he gave me:

Spirits live on in New Orleans. From ordinary families to Voodoo royalty, marble ovens bake the dead, leaving only bones and ashes.

You'll spend eternity in a saintly place guarded by a cross and roses and locked in with a key. To visit, I only need to walk three rows up and two columns over from Egypt.

SCRAWLED in large block letters unlike the handwriting above were the words in bright red ink:

COME SEE WHERE IT ALL BEGAN

"WHAT IN THE world does it mean? What are marble ovens?" Madeline asked before shushing her daughter. "Athena, Mommy needs to talk to Aunt Samantha. You can watch TV. Yes, I'm serious, go!"

I heard her yell, "Yeah!" and then her little footsteps trailed off. I wished I was there to cuddle with her on the couch and watch endless episodes of mindless cartoons.

"It means the mausoleums here. People say the heat bakes the bodies inside the tombs."

"The oven part makes sense, but what does Egypt have to do with a graveyard?"

I pulled out Andrew's cemetery book and searched for Egypt in the index.

"I've got it. Would you believe the actor Nicolas Cage built a pyramid-shaped mausoleum in St. Louis Cemetery

No. 1? And the graveyard is also the final resting place of Marie Laveau, the Voodoo queen."

"That town is crazy." Madeline laughed, but her voice turned serious once again. "So the paper says to go to that graveyard, but you can't do that, Samantha. Not after what you've told me. You need to come home!"

San Francisco wasn't home; New Orleans was home. I couldn't leave without knowing what was waiting at the cemetery. Not that I wanted to leave New Orleans at all.

"Madeline, I can't come back. I must know what's going on here. You understand, don't you?"

The silence at the other end of the phone told me she didn't. Madeline finally spoke. "I guess I understand you want answers. Damn you and all your mysteries."

"You know me, the older version of Nancy Drew."

"Just promise you won't go out by yourself. I want you to live to be as old as Miss Marple."

"I plan to be as old as her, but not with that gray hair."

"I'm serious. Promise you won't go out alone."

"I promise," I lied. "I'll figure it out tomorrow."

"Good, make sure you call me and tell me what you found. And reach out to your friends there. They sound like a great bunch. You don't have to do anything alone."

I lied again to Madeline and promised I would talk to my friends first. I ended the call and looked over the diary page again.

It shouldn't have surprised me that the last entry would end with a visit to a cemetery, but the final sentence confused me. I didn't expect a graveyard to be the start of a story, just the ending.

I knew where to go, but it was already 9:30 p.m., so the cemetery was closed. I was too late to save Kelly and Matt, but what if someone else was there dying? Logic said I should wait for the morning or call the detectives now. Sissy was with Rob and she would make him take me seriously. But what if we found nothing at the tomb?

I didn't believe that for one minute. Somebody took the time to create the diary, place it in my apartment to lead me around the French Quarter. And I couldn't forget about Kelly and Matt. Their deaths made no sense, and I needed a resolution. The only way was to continue following the clues. I had to do it, and I had to do it immediately.

Like Madeline said, I should have asked for help, but I didn't want to risk ruining the relationships I had rebuilt. If I dragged everyone out in the middle of the night on a wild-goose chase, would they ever trust me? I was earning Libby and Neal's trust again. If there was nothing at the graveyard, my credibility would be gone. They would think I made this whole diary up. I'm sure Detective Gammon would put me on the top of the suspect list for both murders, if I wasn't already on it.

I didn't want to be accused of murder or anything else in this horrible drama. I didn't want to lose these friendships, this family.

This mystery needed a solution. If I followed my gut, I would find out who was telling me a story through the diary. I needed the truth first before I put the life I was building in jeopardy. I had no choice but to go to St. Louis Cemetery and follow the clues for one last time.

51

Although the voice of reason tried to speak, I ignored it as I ransacked my kitchen for tools for my cemetery break-in. When Libby said it was a furnished apartment, she wasn't kidding. In a drawer, I found a flashlight with backup batteries and stashed it in my backpack.

I also grabbed a screwdriver and pliers, but I put them back. I didn't think they would help me open a padlock. Climbing over the wall was my best, if not the only option.

I added a pair of kitchen rubber gloves since I didn't have any others to protect my hands, so I wouldn't leave fingerprints. I included a trash bag to my kit to collect evidence or my vomit. The stomach acid creeping up my throat made me think it would be the latter.

As I threw on a black running jacket, the diary key swung around my neck. Maybe I wouldn't need any of my tools, and the key would unlock the gates to the cemetery. Not likely, but weirder things had happened to me in the past few weeks. I tucked the necklace back under my shirt and pulled the hood up on my coat. Very burglary chic, I laughed out loud. The absurdity of my plan tried to take over, but I fought it. Logic wasn't playing a part in my evening plans.

I picked up Andrew's cemetery book and flipped to the chapter on St. Louis No. 1. Just like Andrew, the section was thorough and included a map which showed the tombs in a grid pattern. I grabbed a pen and circled the pyramid and then ripped the page. Along with the new diary entry, I put the map in my backpack now burglary bag.

I closed the courtyard gate behind me and stared longingly at Thibodeaux Mansion. While I had only lived here for a short time, it seemed like home. My neighbors were my family, a family I couldn't bear to lose. My hood slipped off my head as I adjusted my backpack, feeling its weight along with my heavy heart.

Before I lost my nerve, I hurried down the street toward the cemetery, hoping I would find a resolution to this nightmare. Would this be the end of the diary or of me?

52

The front gate for St. Louis was closed with industrial strength chains held together by a large, shiny silver padlock, so the antique key around my neck didn't unlock the cemetery.

"Come back in the morning with a tour group. Marie Laveau needs her beauty sleep." The security guard cackled as he strolled passed the front gate where I stood.

I watched as he walked toward the other end of the graveyard. With his dark uniform stretching over a sizable belly and only a large flashlight hanging from his belt, I was confident I could outrun him if I met him in the cemetery. I thought about calling him back to sweet-talk him into letting me inside, but I was sure he'd heard every excuse and had all kinds of offers to open the gates.

I paced up and down the sidewalk trying to come up with a plan. I then turned the corner on Conti Street to look for another gate that might take my key. I gasped as I saw the walls on this side stood half the height of the front walls. Climbing was my way in.

I grasped the top of the brick wall and tried pulling

myself up. Perhaps if I'd done those pull-ups in my high school gym class, I would have been able to get up the wall. My uncoordinated self dropped to the ground on the outside of the cemetery, not the inside.

I muffled my cries despite the pain. While swinging my arms to check for damage, I scanned the area for other pedestrians. The streetlight cast a yellow glow on the cars and trucks lining the road, but I was alone.

My furnished apartment didn't include climbing supplies, and what I brought wouldn't help me over the high walls. I wasn't ready to give up, so I kept searching for a way in. I came across another doorway, but it had the same chains and lock as the front gate.

I turned from the gate and spotted an overflowing pickup truck parked a few feet away. I crossed my fingers, hoping for a ladder, but no such luck. The empty fruit and vegetable cartons weren't sturdy enough to stand on. Stacking the handful of garbage bags wouldn't work either.

As I looked for another vehicle, a thud on top of the bags made me jump. I laughed seeing it was only a cat.

"Are you a friend of Cleopatra and Nefertiti?" I asked as I stroked her back and searched for a collar. She didn't have one, but she had a circle of white fur on top of her head that made her identifiable and unique. She appeared healthy as her black coat shone in the moonlight. If she was homeless, she took good care of herself.

From the way she pawed at the garbage bags, I assumed that's how she fed herself. As she ripped open a bag, I noticed a milk crate underneath it.

"Hey, pretty girl, you need to move, please," I said to the purring cat while I pushed the bags aside to uncover three crates. "You are my good luck charm!"

My new friend jumped out of the truck and slinked away

as cats do after they've accomplished their goals. Did a guardian angel send her? Someone was looking out for me, at least of the furry persuasion.

I carried the crates to the wall, placing two on the ground and one on top like a pyramid. I stepped on the top crate, planting my feet to see if it would hold me. I shook from fear, not from the unstable crates. The sturdy setup gave me enough height to look over the wall to discover that there was just a few feet in between two mausoleums for me to fit. I hoped.

I took a deep breath and put my hands on top of the wall, but my whole body shuddered and my breathing hastened. In this shape, there was no way I would get over safely or quietly.

Using the crates as a chair, I evaluated my situation. I could go home and come back tomorrow as a tourist. Or I could beg the security guard to let me in. Or I could reach out to a friend, but whom?

Not William or Libby or I would lose their confidence and most likely my apartment. Neal was out of the question as we just became friends again. Joey might help, but I didn't know him as well as the others. Connor would come if he wasn't at the restaurant, but our relationship might not survive a late-night breaking-and-entering call. Frankie wouldn't be able to climb over a brick wall, but she would send Frank to help. I didn't trust him, though.

I would have asked Sissy for help, but as a medical professional and a detective's girlfriend, she might be legally, if not morally, obligated to tell Rob. As supportive of a friend as she was to me, I couldn't see her agreeing to my plan. I didn't want to put her in a difficult situation; I also didn't want to lose her friendship.

Last, but not least, was Andrew, whom I trusted as much

as Sissy. He knew the cemetery best so he would be a great help. Also, he would have an outfit worthy of burglary chic.

The hard part now was what to text Andrew. After a few false starts, I typed:

Hey. This sounds crazy but I'm at the cemetery because I got another diary entry. It's probably fake, but I'm checking it out tonight. If you get this, text me or come find me here. Watch out for the security guard. Thanks.

My finger hovered over the send button, my fear of appearing insane causing me to hesitate. I finally sent it, and there was no turning back. If nothing else, at least someone knew where I was if something happened. Also, I had no doubt that Andrew would bail me out for trespassing, if needed.

I stared at my phone, hoping for an instant response, but after waiting the longest five minutes, I had to decide. Either head home and try to forget about the diary for tonight, or climb that wall and follow the murder's instructions.

To keep my friends and find the truth, I didn't have a choice. I stood up, brushed my clammy hands on my jeans, and breathed out. Time to go over that wall.

53

C hanneling the confidence of a world-class athlete, I stepped up on the milk crates ready to perform my acrobatic maneuver into the cemetery. I lifted my right leg over first and twisted my body so I hung partially over the wall facing outward. I swung my left leg over and held on to the top of the wall with my sweaty hands.

My relief of making it over the side disappeared as I lost my grip. Instead of gracefully dropping, I fell like dead weight. "Shit!" I yelled without thinking before jumping up and flattening myself against a tomb.

I gritted my teeth so I wouldn't make any more noise. Checking myself for injuries, I only found streaks of stucco from the tombs on my coat and jeans. I broke nothing except my pride.

Using the flashlight app on my phone, I looked at my surroundings. The mausoleums surrounding me stood about six feet tall with bits of their brick infrastructure showing through crumbling white plaster. The roof and walls were plain, but Andrew's book stated that any decorations would be on the façade along with the family name.

Fractured concrete dotted the hard ground, so I carefully maneuvered my way to the front of the tomb. I almost screamed when I brushed up against a fern growing from the wall. Plants sprouted from cracks in the mortar, impressing me with their ability to thrive without soil. The rainy New Orleans climate must help, but did they also get nutrients from the dead? The image of ferns and vines growing in and out of bodies wasn't what I needed. Time to toughen up and not let foliage scare me or the guard would hear my outbursts.

Where was he anyway? Taking a chance, I edged out until I heard a voice singing, "Freaks come out at night. Freaks come out at night."

I whipped my body back around and flattened myself against the tomb as the security guard passed. He must sing an album's worth of spooky-themed songs on his rounds. The jarring ring of a cell phone interrupted his crooning.

He stopped and answered it, so I had no choice but to wait while he chatted a few feet away from me.

"Hey, sweetie. Yes, I'm working. No, I haven't seen the Voodoo queen tonight." His laughter filled the air, and for a moment I relaxed along with him. "A few minutes ago I would have said nothing's going on, but I might be wrong."

I held my breath and tried not to move.

"I smell smoke. It's real faint, but I'll head to the front to check it out. Maybe it's a new food truck. I would love something besides a Lucky Dog…"

His voice trailed off, and I exhaled. Sniffing the air, I caught a slight scent of burning wood. Perhaps New Orleans barbecue differed from the infrequent barbecue joints or cookouts I'd attended. Whatever the case, I needed to take advantage of the guard's distraction. My pounding chest and acidic stomach were killing me, but I pulled the diary page and map from my bag and got to work.

A large, round four-story monument stood ten feet in front of me. Between its size and elegant statues I spotted it easily on the map, and it gave me my bearings. The pyramid tomb was two rows and two columns over. I would find it first and then get to the mausoleum I needed from there.

If I didn't run into the security guard, or break my ankle on uneven ground, or meet the spirit of Marie Laveau, I would be fine. As I crept around, I hoped my feet would keep me upright and my heavy breathing wouldn't give me away. The moonlight shone enough to light my way through most of the cemetery, although a few missteps on deteriorating graves made me wish for my flashlight.

While it felt like hours, in less than two minutes I faced the pyramid. I crouched down in front of it to catch my breath and listen for the singing security guard. I didn't hear him so hopefully he was enjoying a long, hearty meal. The scent of burning wood was stronger here. It could have been my nervous stomach, but the smoke was neither comforting nor inviting like I would expect from a food truck. At least a high quality one.

"Tiptoe through the graves," I sang in my head as I started toward my destination. The guard wasn't the only person who could carry a tune in the cemetery. I followed the directions and crept three rows up and two rows over from the pyramid and paused at the row from the diary.

In this section, the mausoleums all looked alike. The only solution was to inspect each one for a cross with roses, and that would take time since there were at least a dozen to check. I bit my lip in frustration. Hoping I was doing it right,

I made the sign of the cross and began my search. My new furry friend sauntered out from behind a mausoleum, interrupting my hunt.

"Hey, sweet kitty. Is this your family?" I murmured as I stared at the dilapidated tomb she appeared from. It wasn't the right vault, so I tried to walk. The cat meowed at me before I took a step, so I bent over to pet her. My key necklace hung from my neck, and she batted it like a toy.

"I'm an idiot," I whispered after giving her one last head rub. "It's all about the key. Thanks."

My key was all I needed.

I picked up my pace and searched for a mausoleum with a lock. At the end of the row stood a tomb topped with a large cross intertwined with roses. Relief washed over me when I saw a door with a keyhole on the left-hand side of the tomb and a nameplate on the right.

I couldn't read the worn family name etched on the top. There were no vines or ferns growing out of this tomb, as the plaster covering it was pristine. From the faded name, it must have been an older grave site, but well taken care of over the years.

Touching the keyhole, it surprised me to find a bit of oil on my fingers. Between the clean condition of the outside and the lubricated lock, I couldn't help but think someone opened the tomb recently. I shivered at the thought of finding another body. And if it was empty, then this wild-goose chase was worth it in that I would know this was a joke. More importantly, I wouldn't have ruined any of my friendships over this ridiculous ordeal.

I took off my necklace, but my hand froze in midair. Was I prepared for what would happen once I opened the door?

The graveyard kitty thought I was ready as she gave one

last meow before backing away and scurrying off. Did she know what I would find?

Part of me wanted to run like the cat, but I turned the key, and the click told me all I needed to know.

I was at the right tomb.

The voice behind me confirmed it.

"Welcome home, baby sis."

54

I recognized the voice. I suspected all my friends of being the diary writer and murderer, but I didn't want it to be true. If only I could tap my heels three times and wish myself home.

But I was home.

"Aren't you going to say hello?"

"Hi, Joey."

I turned around to face the man I'd assumed I'd met only a few weeks ago. Apparently we'd met before, at my birth. He was my brother, but he waited until we were trespassing in the middle of a cemetery to share that fact with me.

"Fancy meeting you here," I joked. In my head my voice sounded lighthearted, but out loud we both heard the fear spilling out with each word.

"It is a surprise, isn't it?" he said as he moved closer to me. "I figured we'd meet up here tomorrow after you read the diary page, but you came right out here."

"How did you know?"

"I put an app on your phone to track you. The night at

The Gas Light when you asked everyone to give you their numbers, I installed it. You're a little too trusting."

His grin made me shudder even more than the cold tone of his voice.

"Why are we here? Why did you say this is where it all began?"

"Because, baby sister, this is where our second lives began. Our first lives ended after Hurricane Geoffrey killed our parents and supposedly you. Look, here's your name."

Joey pointed at the last words engraved on the tomb: *Sawyer Ford, Anna Grace, and Sarah Jane St. Martin, perished on August 17, 1990.*

The tears welling up in my eyes made it hard to see the names, so I reached out to touch them. I traced the letters, wishing it would impart memories of these people, of me. Worn names on a cold marble slab provided no information. I needed Joey for that even though standing with him brought me no peace.

"I am Sarah."

"Yes, you are. I'm Samuel Joseph St. Martin. I switched to Joey Martin when I came to New Orleans in case you remembered your brother's name."

"You're Samuel? Sam?"

"Funny, isn't it? You being Samantha now."

His laugh echoed off the surrounding tombs, but I didn't laugh along with him. My soul ached at his revelation. The two-year-old child found on the side of the highway after the hurricane hadn't been saying her own name; she was calling for her brother.

"Everyone said Sarah Jane, meaning you, died during the storm, but I knew better." His voice cracked, but he regained his composure. "They told me it wasn't my fault. I should have protected you, and for that I'm sorry. But even though you're here in New Orleans, you don't care about your real family. Did you ever?"

"Yes, I did! It's one reason I moved here," I insisted. "But if you're my brother, why didn't you tell me? How long have you known?"

"My uncle told me. I lived with him, our aunt, and two cousins in Mississippi after the storm. About a year ago, I found my uncle drunk, well, drunker than usual, on the porch. He complained that his money tree had died in a car wreck."

Joey paused, and I wasn't sure if it was for dramatic effect or he'd noticed I was trembling. I didn't want to hear the rest of his story, but I needed to listen.

"He said to me, 'I guess I might as well tell you, your sister is alive,' and he laughed and laughed." Joey appeared to be reliving the night as his voice grew rougher and he clenched his fists. "He was in Baton Rouge when he saw you with your adopted parents. He blackmailed them, so he and our aunt wouldn't claim you. Not that they wanted another mouth to feed."

My parents' behavior now made sense. I now understood why we never returned to Louisiana and why they refused to talk about my past. They had to keep silent to keep me. They paid the price of losing their past to hide mine.

"Why didn't you find me once you knew I was alive?"

"It wasn't so easy. It took some time after my uncle's funeral to find the paperwork he had on you. Oh, yes, Uncle Preston had an accident that night. He fell off the porch, hit his head, and died that night."

Joey's crooked smile made it quite clear it was no accident.

"How do I know you're not lying? What proof do you have that I'm your missing sister?"

"Not going to take my word for it? Fine, look at these."

He came over and shoved a handful of papers into my hands. Shining a flashlight over me, I heard Joey's deep breaths as I looked through them. The birth certificate for Sarah Jane St. Martin and my birth certificate didn't persuade me as anyone could have them. The copies of checks my parents wrote to a Preston St. Martin from the year of my adoption to the month before they died did convince me. And the copy of the same photo my mother had hidden away was the final nail in the coffin.

"Do you believe me now? See, your selfish parents kept you from your real family."

I wanted to defend them, but I couldn't speak. Trying to keep down the confusion and anger I felt toward my parents, I breathed in deeply. Now wasn't the time to explain my parents to Joey. I needed more answers about the rest of the story, my story. After handing him the papers, I found my voice.

"How did you find me?"

"Where else? On social media. I tried to think of a way to contact you. Saying hi, your adopted parents lied to you, and I'm your brother didn't seem right."

"No, it wouldn't have been good."

"I kept looking at your Instagram and Facebook posts, learning about you and working on my approach, when I found out you were moving to New Orleans."

"Basically, you stalked me and then followed me here."

"It sounds creepy when you say it like that." He grinned. "Did you think the diary was creepy, too?"

"It was fun at first..."

"See, I knew you'd like it! I read on your Facebook page

how you liked mysteries, scavenger hunts, and romantic comedies, so I was sure you wouldn't be able to resist reading it. Momma loved those things, too."

Joey sat down next to me on the step. He brushed a slight smudge of dirt off the front of the mausoleum, then pressed his hand against the name, Anna Grace. "Hey, Momma, your babies are back together."

His face softened as he said her name, and for a moment, I recognized the man whom I'd grown to like over the past few weeks. The Joey I'd spent time with was funny and charming, a guy who checked in on a new friend, and brought her pralines.

"Joey, what happened during the storm?"

He sat, tapping his right foot on the patch of dirt. Part of me wanted to reach out and put my hand on his leg to stop him from moving, but that would have been a comforting gesture. He hadn't earned my sympathy, but maybe he would after he spoke.

"A few months before the hurricane, we moved to New Orleans. Momma and Pop wanted to go back to where our family was from originally. When the storm started, Momma thought it would be safer to ride it out back in Mississippi, so we left. The car broke down near the Louisiana and Mississippi border, and as we walked to get help, the wind raged around us."

Even though he was recounting an event from almost thirty years ago, the tension and sadness in his voice made it seem like it happened yesterday.

"We held on to each other, but your doll, your damn BB doll, slipped out of your hand. You ran back for it, and the winds and rain sent us in all different directions. I ended up on the Mississippi side of the highway. They recovered

Momma and Pop's bodies a few months later. They didn't find your body, so you were declared dead."

"But you didn't think I was dead," I whispered. My history was revealed. I had a family who hadn't abandoned me. Surprised by the tears streaming down my face, I used my jacket sleeves to wipe them away.

I remembered Andrew questioning whether it was worse to know your past or not know. I had an answer for him now: knowing was worse.

"No, I would have felt it if you were dead. We were as close as any brother and sister could be, Sarah Jane. Don't you remember? We played hide-and-seek all the time, and you hated to lose! I was teaching you to play the piano before the hurricane. And I always bought you pralines."

I closed my eyes and let my mind wander to my childhood before my adoption. I prayed I would recall Joey, Samuel, whoever he had been to me.

Nothing came to me. Nothing at all.

"Joey, I mean, Sam, I wish you had just told me who you were when I got here instead of leaving the diary and the dolls."

"It's too late now. I thought you'd figure out the clues and it would be a fun scavenger hunt, a good way to remember our past. Instead, it turned into murder, and it's your fault."

55

"My fault? How did I turn it into murder?" I demanded. Receiving confirmation that the diary writer and murderer were the same brought me, the amateur detective, no joy.

"I had to kill Kelly because she tried to interrupt the game. I used her to try out the riddles. She seemed to like them, so I assumed you would, too. But when she caught us together, she wanted to meet y'all."

"I wasn't crazy; she yelled for you that night. But why did she call you Sam?"

"Thank God she did or everyone would have known she knew me," he said. "On our first date, she saw my real name on my license. I told her I had to use a different identity because I had warrants out for speeding tickets. She was so desperate for a boyfriend she bought my story."

"Her friends said she really cared for you, but she was just a silly woman to you," I snapped.

"I actually liked her, and I would have introduced her to you, but she wouldn't wait until we finished the diary clues."

I jumped as Joey slapped his hand against the tomb.

"I took her to the house for the riddle and tried to explain that I created a treasure hunt for a friend, but she accused me of lying. She said she'd find the truth even if she had to follow me around the Quarter. I couldn't let her do that so I grabbed a pipe and hit her. I hadn't planned to kill her. Sarah Jane, I promise you that."

Joey, or Sam, whatever he called himself, reached down and held my hands and looked me in the eyes. Was this part of his act or the truth?

"I brought the BB doll with me to leave for you in the house, so I just changed my plans and left it for you with Kelly's body. I assumed it would shake things up. You weren't getting any of my hints."

He let go of my hands. "You are Sarah Jane. You are my baby sister."

The increasing winds blew faded ribbons and withered flower petals from the tomb across the row. I reached out to grab a long pink ribbon for something tangible to hold on to as Joey stared at me. This conversation was becoming an out-of-body experience, and I needed an object to ground me, although mementos from a grave weren't ideal. As I twirled the ribbon around my fingers, I spoke.

"If you didn't plan to kill her, what about Matt? He was our friend. Your friend!"

"Was he? He put up with me because of Neal. Once again, you post everything online, so I learned where you were moving. I found the building and made friends with the guys. Neal's an easy mark. Buy that man a beer and he's a friend for life!"

Joey's laughter annoyed me more than I expected, and I stood up to confront him. "Neal is a great person and so was Matt. Explain what happened. Did he figure out what you were up to?"

"Finally! You're acting like a detective," he said. "He saw me the day I put the diary in your apartment. He never really believed me when I told him I was helping Libby move furniture. That last night he called me out when I walked past his office. He said he would tell you I was in your place and also that he thought I lied about Kelly. I couldn't convince him he was wrong, so I did what I had to do."

"You killed him," I said. He was right about Matt's death. It was my fault. The ribbon slipped from my hand as I sank back onto the cold step and rested my head on my shaking knees. Biting the inside of my cheek to keep my teeth from chattering, I finally looked up at the murderer's face.

"I had no choice. Matt would have told the police I murdered Kelly. And you still didn't know your name. I needed more time. I needed tonight."

"And here we are. Now what?"

"Oh, Sarah Jane. You've had the key all along."

<h1 style="text-align:center">56</h1>

I had the tomb key, but did I have the key to their murders all along? Could I have prevented their deaths? As much as I wanted to run away from this cold graveyard and dark story, I needed to understand what Joey meant.

"Once again, you're confused, baby sis." He sighed as he walked back in front of me. "I can't believe you're this clueless still."

Yes, I was confused, and I didn't need to confirm it with words. His disappointment was palpable.

"I assumed you'd figure everything out from the diary. Like Napoleon House was our family's favorite restaurant, and the museum was to remind you of our first, and only, Mardi Gras season."

His voice softened as he continued, "At every parade, Pop set you on his shoulders, and you screamed at people to throw you stuff. Momma and I grabbed the beads and put them around your neck. You just loved it."

I smiled at his sweet story, but the memories of a two-year-old me didn't appear. My reaction appeared to encourage him as he kept going.

"See, you're starting to remember! Momma made artwork with the trinkets she talked you into giving her. The cottage I sent you to was like the one we lived in where Momma filled every nook and cranny with her projects. And Pop played the piano while I sang and you danced…"

My smile must have waned because he stopped reminiscing and pulled me up from the step. "You don't know what I'm talking about, do you? Not one damn thing?"

"Joey, I wish I did, really I do. It sounds so amazing, but I was two! How could I? Who knows what happened to me during the hurricane?" I tried to explain, but his frantic pacing and shaking head told me it wasn't working.

"You should remember! You loved me!" he yelled.

Why didn't his screaming bring the security guard over here? The wind picked up again, but I didn't smell the smoke anymore. The guard should have wrapped up his meal by now, if a food truck had produced the smoke.

"I'm sorry."

"Are you sorry? I don't believe you," he said as he kicked at a bare patch of dirt.

"I don't know if I can ever apologize enough for you, Joey, I mean, Sam. But where do we go from here?" Out of this cemetery is where I wanted to go. I scanned the nearby tombs for anything that could be a weapon. The plastic vases wouldn't do any damage and I didn't think I could pick up and then throw any of the decorative marble angels or urns.

"Well, baby sis, my original plan had us visiting the family tomb after you finished the scavenger hunt, as a kind of rebirth. That's why I left the key with the diary because it's your birthright."

Joey mumbled to himself as he stomped back and forth in front of me. I craned my neck to look for the security guard one last time before I tried to escape. Between Joey's tirade and his increasingly agitated manner, I had to get out of there. There would be no happy ending in his story.

"Where are you going, Sarah Jane? We're not done here," Joey growled as I turned to make a run for it.

He grabbed my arm and yanked me back toward him. Pulling away from him didn't work, as he was bigger, stronger, and angrier than me, although my anger started to outweigh my fear as he pushed me over to the tomb.

"You need to meet Momma and Pop."

He finished turning the key and opened the St. Martin crypt. Before I screamed, my brother covered my mouth and the marble door swung open.

57

The tomb was empty.

Joey released me, snickering as he stepped back from the opening. I moved closer to see inside the mausoleum. It contained three marble shelves covered in a fine film. Bone dust or dirt, I didn't want to know.

"Did you expect corpses with rotting flesh?" he asked. "It only takes about a year for the bodies to decay. Momma and Pop were the last ones entombed."

"Where are they?"

"The bones get brushed down to the bottom so they can place in the newest coffin. It's very efficient."

I nodded my head while speculating why it was empty.

"I guess you're wondering why it's cleaned out. See, I've been thinking. Like I said, Plan A was we would meet here to start our second life together. We had so much time to make up for, baby sis!"

He put his arm around me, but the tightness of his grip was not loving or kind. "I kept hoping and praying that you'd remember something, anything. When we sat in your kitchen eating pralines, I expected you to tell me you remembered your past, but instead you said you were done searching. That your friends were more important than your birth family."

I knew my lies would catch up with me, but I didn't think this lie would be the one to get me into trouble. Telling Joey I was putting off my search for my birth parents had been the wrong thing to say to him. That afternoon had been my last chance to save myself from whatever he had planned. I shivered, wondering what was next to come.

As he began pacing again, I took stock of my predicament. Would my voice carry through the graveyard? Even if the guard heard me, would he be of any help? Joey had already killed at least two people, and I didn't want to be responsible for another death. Maybe I could defuse the situation; otherwise, I just needed to run like hell when I got the chance.

"Joey, Sam, we can still start over. We have all the time in the world," I lied. "Let's go back to my apartment and finish the pralines you brought over. I want to learn all about your life."

"My life? It was miserable and lonely without you and Momma and Pop," he said. "You had new parents, and now you have a new family here. You don't need me."

"But I want us to be a family. I promise," I fibbed again. "Let me show you. I keep a copy of that photo you showed me in my wallet, so I do care. It's not too late."

I took my backpack off and placed it on the ground. I pretended to look for my wallet, but I texted Sissy a quick message. Hopefully *911 St Louis* would make sense to her.

"Are you lying?"

"No, here it is." I handed the picture to Joey. He looked at it briefly and threw it down. A strong wind blew through the cemetery and carried the photo away along with my hopes of changing Joey's mind.

"It's too late. I don't believe a damn word from you, and your actions over the past weeks told me all I needed to know," he said as he reached beside the doorway for something I couldn't see as the moonlight had shifted.

"If you won't be Sarah Jane now, be the old Sarah Jane. She belongs in the mausoleum with the rest of the family. Everyone else thinks you're dead. I'm just going to make it the truth."

I made a run for it again, but only got a few feet before Joey grabbed my hood and pulled me backward. As I struggled to get out of his grasp, he struck me on the side of my head. I collapsed onto the marble step in front of the mausoleum. My eyes wouldn't focus as a headache overtook me, but I was still conscious. I crawled on the ground, but it felt like I had a two-hundred-pound weight on my back.

"Sarah Jane, stop trying to move. You're not going anywhere. You did this all the time when I used to put you down for a nap."

I felt myself being lifted into the air and then pushed onto a cold, hard surface. I started coughing from the dust and a horrid smell I couldn't identify. The pain in my head grew as I squirmed back and forth, struggling to find a comfortable position. My eyes refused to stay open; I just wanted to rest.

"Sarah Jane, are you cozy in there? Ready for your nap? Should I sing you a lullaby?"

"Sam, I need my dolly. Where's my dolly?" I whined. "I can't go night-night without her."

"What? What did you say? Are you playing with me? Why did you ask for the damn doll now?"

I drifted off to sleep to those words...

58

W hy can't I sit up?
  Why is it so dark?
  My head is pounding.
Is it a migraine?
It smells disgusting.
Did I throw up in my bed?
Was that blood dripping down my face?
As I banged my head for the second time on a hard surface, I remembered. I, Sarah Jane St. Martin, was lying in my family crypt. Back where it began, according to Joey, sorry, make that Sam.

For my entire life I had assumed my birth family was gone, but I had a brother who never gave up on my existence. Unfortunately, he now wanted me dead.

Damn, why won't my head stop throbbing? Do I have a concussion? I'm not supposed to sleep if I have one. Breathe in, breathe out. Stay awake!

My eyes closed once again, and I could feel my body ready to fall asleep. I bit the inside of my cheek to keep myself awake. If I wanted to escape, I had to pull myself together. I had to figure a way out of this marble oven before I ran out of oxygen. The prospect of suffocating caused me to breathe even heavier, and my heart raced. My hysterical laughter filled the tomb as I remembered the name of a yoga pose: corpse pose.

After my hysterics, I recalled how calming that position felt, and tried to replicate it. Lying still and clearing my mind enabled me to slow my breathing and pulse.

"Namaste," I whispered as I let the calmness wash over me.

Ignoring my headache, I scooted down to the end of the shelf and banged my feet against the solid door. Nothing happened except new pains ran up and down my legs. Using my feet again, I searched for a latch or handle to open the door, but no luck. Apparently tombs didn't include safety features for people buried alive.

Humor helped for a moment, but it wouldn't get me out of the mausoleum. My backpack was lying next to my hip, so I reached in to grab the flashlight.

I concentrated on my breathing again as the reality of my situation came into focus. From the vaulted ceiling, I realized I was on the top shelf of the tomb. I had just enough space to roll over. I discovered a rectangular opening behind my head. Hope left me once I remembered the hole was the slot to brush the bone dust down to the bottom of the crypt. That wasn't the way I wanted to leave the vault.

I reached into the bag and clutched my phone. Joey must have forgotten it or he assumed there was no reception inside a thick marble mausoleum. He was right. No service. And no response from Andrew or Sissy, but that didn't mean they didn't get my message. I had to keep fighting until they got here...if they could find me.

Wishing I had brought the tools from my kitchen, I used

the flashlight to bang against the walls. The side of the flashlight cracked, and the light went out. I banged the broken light down in frustration. I would die before I dented the wall.

"Help! Someone help me!" I screamed while I once again scooted down the shelf to pound my feet on the door of the tomb. If I was going to die, I would go out as a fighter. I was Samantha Richardson, not the dead Sarah Jane St. Martin. I wanted to leave this world as the person I was, not the child Joey called me.

It seemed like hours of banging, but it must have only been minutes. My legs ached, but it couldn't compete with the constant throbbing in my head. The volume of my voice grew lower with each weak hit against the impenetrable door.

I wanted to give up, but I convinced myself I just needed a quick break. As I closed my eyes and wrapped my arms around my shaking body, I tried again to recreate the calm of corpse pose. Gasping in the stale tomb air, and rocking side to side, didn't put me in a peaceful state of body or mind. As I turned to lie on my stomach, I licked the tears that ran down my cheeks, thinking they would be the only water I drank before I died on the cold hard shelf.

Not being a religious person, I never gave much thought to the afterlife. Would my parents be waiting for me? I would have two sets of parents to welcome me, if I was going to heaven and not hell. But I was already in hell, lying in this vault.

No, I wasn't going to hell, at least not yet. Thoughts of the friends, of the family, I had made in my short time in New Orleans filled my head instead of fears of dying. Joey needed to be held accountable for Kelly's and Matt's deaths. I wouldn't let him be responsible for mine.

With renewed energy I grasped the broken flashlight and banged on the walls. I put it down and picked up my cell phone, waving it around in hopes of finding a signal. Screaming until my voice was raw and my headache was too much to bear, I finally set my phone down.

I wasn't ready to give up, but I needed to rest. Just a few minutes of sleep and I would start again. By then I bet Andrew and Sissy would find me and it would be all right...

A cool breeze washed over me. A light illuminated the tomb. I shouldn't have been surprised; supposedly, there is a bright light to lead the dearly departed to the afterlife.

I was dead. The voice of an angel called me, but didn't welcome me to heaven.

"Sammy! Don't die on us, honey! We've got you!"

Even with bright flashlights blurring my vision, along with my pounding headache, I recognized Sissy's voice.

"Connor and Neal, pull her out gently. Now, Andrew, spread my coat out so they can put her down on it. I need to assess her injuries, and she can't stay in there."

Four hands were on my body, dragging me out and placing me on the hard yet comforting ground. I gasped for air, keeping my eyes closed as I still wasn't sure if I was dead or alive.

"Sammy! Look at me! Open your eyes!" Sissy demanded.

I opened my eyes on command, and I wouldn't have been surprised if the bodies in the surrounding graves did the same. Sissy's authority had no bounds.

"Good. Now, can you say your name? Do you know who I am?"

I took in one more deep breath and exhaled slowly before answering, "I'm Samantha but you call me Sammy. And you're Sissy."

My friends all started speaking at once. Sissy's voice

stopped them. "Yes, we're all happy she's alive, but listen to me."

Andrew, Connor, and Neal stood still and listened to Sissy's instructions.

"Go to the front and tell the police we found her and to send the paramedics back here. She might have a concussion, and she's going into shock. Run!" She pointed to Neal who tried to speak, but Sissy yelled, "Go now!" so he gave me the thumbs-up sign and ran.

"Guys, give me your coats so we can keep her warm."

"Thanks," I said as Connor put his on me first.

"Of course," he said and kissed me on the cheek. "You'll be okay."

Andrew placed his coat on me next and bit his lip before he spoke. "My dear, I'm overjoyed you texted me, but you should have called. I don't text."

I tried to laugh but coughed instead. "Sorry, I forgot."

"I'm only teasing you. I am glad you contacted me," he said while patting my hand.

"I got your text just when Andrew called me, and we figured out you were here," Sissy said. "Can you tell us what happened?"

"We're confused how you got in the tomb," Connor said. "Andrew grabbed me and Neal and we met Sissy and Rob here. I get that you were following the diary, but how did you get in there?"

I dug my fingers into the cool mixture of dirt and grass that I lay on. I needed to hold on to the earth to remind myself I was out of the tomb and surrounded by friends, not dust and memories. Sissy grasped my wrist again to take my pulse and looked at me with such concern that I had to speak.

"First, tell me how you found me? Could you hear me in there?"

"Okay, well, no, we couldn't," Connor answered. "We rushed into the cemetery after the guard let us in. I ran into Joey who pointed me down this row."

"I was close by and heard them talking," Andrew said. "Joey told me he heard noises and would get a crowbar from the security office."

"Joey ran so fast I couldn't ask him any questions," Connor said.

"As Connor and I searched, there was a mournful cry. I assumed it was you, but to my surprise a black cat was sitting on the step of this tomb," Andrew said. "Very dramatic, I must say."

"The cat stopped meowing and ran off as soon as we ran over," Connor said. "I pointed out the key in the lock, and Andrew recognized it as the one you've been wearing."

"I came flying up after," Sissy replied as she checked me over. Her face grew serious. My pulse must have been through the roof since I could feel my heart beating.

"When we opened it, there you were. Now will you tell us how you got in there?" Andrew asked.

I sat up even though Sissy tried to push me gently back down. Even with my strained voice and pounding head, I needed them to know the truth.

I whispered, "Joey put me in there."

"What did you say, Sammy?" Connor asked as he kneeled closer to me. "Did you say Joey?"

"Yes! Joey! Joey is my brother!"

60

Before my friends could react to my revelation, Neal and Rob rushed down the aisle with the EMTs. Sissy directed the paramedics while Andrew and Connor grabbed the detectives. The medical team blocked my view, so the last thing I saw was Rob and his partner rushing away with Neal and Connor following them.

Just as they lifted me on the gurney, my furry friend from earlier strolled out from behind the tomb. She jumped on the stretcher and curled up next to my face, purring in my ear.

"Ma'am, is this your cat?" a paramedic asked while trying to remove her. She sank her claws into the sheet covering me.

I removed the oxygen mask to reply, "She is now."

Looking confused, Andrew grabbed the cat who released her claws as I told her, "Go with Uncle Andrew. I'll meet you at home."

"Did you know she had a pet?" he said. Sissy shook her head. "I guess I'm taking this creature to Thibodeaux Mansion."

Before I could explain, the paramedics insisted I put the mask back on. As we reached the front gate, I was relieved to see the singing security guard talking with Detective Gammon.

"Well, now, this explains why the trash barrels were all on fire on the other side of the cemetery," the guard said as they wheeled me toward him. "Did you light them to distract me? Were you trying to contact Marie Laveau?"

No, I came here for the living.

My brother wanted me dead, but I was coming out alive. But was I leaving as Samantha Richardson or Sarah Jane St. Martin?

61

As I went through a battery of tests at the hospital, I knew I was Samantha Richardson. My head wound needed a few stitches, but physically I was in fair shape. Between the pain medication and the physicality of the evening, I slept soundly. It was the first time since the murders I had a decent night's sleep. All it took was my own attempted murder and narcotics.

When I woke up in the morning, I smiled to see I wasn't alone. Curled up in the only chair was Connor. His snores echoed off the sterile white walls. His bone-dust-tousled hair, and the little trail of drool running from the corner of his mouth made me like him even more. A man that will run through a cemetery at midnight and stay dirty while sleeping by your hospital bed was a keeper.

"My goodness, you're awake! And before Mr. Sleepy-head, too," Sissy chirped as she entered the room carrying a large bouquet of yellow roses, with Andrew and Rob following behind her. "He hasn't left that chair all night."

Connor stirred, then wiped the drool from his face as we

laughed. "Um, good morning to y'all, too. Hey, Sammy. How are you feeling?"

"My headache isn't too bad," I said as I touched the bandage over my stitches. "I'm very lucky. I'll never be able to thank everyone enough for helping me."

Andrew reached over the bed rails to hold my hand. "We will always be here for you. Remember, next time, call us before you do something so outrageous. So we can stop you." He grinned. "Or join you."

"Don't you say that!" Sissy giggled. "Especially in front of Rob."

"Yes, especially in front of me," Rob said, but then he smiled. "Okay, you potential lawbreakers, I need a moment with your leader. Would y'all give Miss Sammy and me a few minutes, please?"

Andrew and Sissy each gave me a quick hug before leaving the room. Connor brushed the hair off my face and kissed me on the lips before he closed the door behind him. I needed all the goodwill I could get as I assumed Rob was there to read me the riot act or arrest me.

Rob settled into the chair and took out his notebook. I braced myself for a lecture, but he said, "Your friends gave me the information you shared with them, but I'd like to hear it firsthand from you."

He listened to the whole story starting from the discovery of the diary page hidden with my parade trinkets to my illegal entry into the cemetery and ending with my confrontation with Joey. My voice cracked when I explained that my birth name was Sarah Jane St. Martin.

"It's okay to be upset. Finding out who you are, or rather was, must be an overwhelming experience."

"I never imagined this was my story."

"This is a first for me, too, and I deal with all kinds of

crazy being a cop," Rob said. "I'm glad you found out about your past, but I'm sorry how Joey shared it with you."

The way Joey, I guess I should call him Sam, revealed my truth horrified me. It could have been a heartwarming reveal with the scavenger hunt, but it led to two murders, almost three. Would anything good ever come from this revelation?

Rob seemed to read my mind. "I'm a spiritual man myself, so I think God brought you here, but whatever the case is, I speak for all of us in that we're glad you're here. I hope you'll remember that as you recover from this event."

"I will," I promised through a trickle of tears as I reached for a box of tissues. "Thank you for being so kind."

"Of course. Now let's discuss some business. First, we have confirmed that Joey is Samuel Joseph St. Martin. He lost his parents and baby sister after Hurricane Geoffrey. We also found this in his apartment. I'm sorry, but it will be hard for you to see."

Rob handed me the same stack of papers that Joey had shown me in the graveyard. It still shocked me that my parents were blackmailed until they died. Even as an adult, they didn't want me to know about my birth family. Would I ever learn if they were afraid of my uncle or if they just wanted me to themselves? My uncle and both sets of parents were dead, and I assumed those answers were buried with them.

"Joey showed them to me last night, so I'm not surprised," I said as I passed them back to Rob. "Well, as surprised as I was last night. Did you find anything else in his apartment? Did you find him?"

"He left a toothbrush and hairbrush on top of the papers. I assume so we could do a DNA test to confirm your relationship."

"He was thorough." I tried to laugh, but it hurt my head and my heart. "I take it he's on the run?"

"We're looking for him, and we have an APB out on him. We contacted his, and I guess, now, your aunt. She confirmed that Joey left a few months back without a word. She hasn't heard from him. And she sounded shocked to find out about you."

"Oh…"

"Don't worry, I didn't give her your contact information even though she asked for it. I told her I'd offer you her number so you could call when you're ready."

"Thank you. I'm not up for meeting another relative right now."

Rob nodded and flipped over another page in his notebook. "You do what you think is best, but in the meantime, we'll keep searching for Joey. It's not over."

I reached over to the water glass beside my bed and took a long sip. I agreed with Rob; it wasn't over. Would Joey try to kill me again? Or was he out of my life once again? I also wanted justice for Kelly and Matt.

"Do you have proof Joey killed Kelly and Matt? He confessed to me, but is that enough?"

"We matched his fingerprints from his apartment to both murder weapons, so when we find him, we'll charge him with their deaths."

"I'm glad to hear that."

"He'll be charged with your attempted murder, too. His prints were on a piece of rebar outside the mausoleum. He didn't strike you as hard as the others or you would be dead. Do you know why?"

"At first I think he wanted me to die in the tomb, so I had time to reflect about what I'd done wrong to him."

"What did you do?"

"I didn't remember him. And then he thought I didn't want to find my birth family."

"But how could you remember? You were just a toddler. And not everyone looks for their birth family."

"I know, but Joey said I was wrong not to remember and wrong to give up my search for my birth family. When I didn't figure out that the clues in the diary were our childhood memories, he decided I should die since Sarah Jane was already dead."

"I'm not sure if that's evil or crazy, but he did leave the key in the lock. And he told Andrew and Connor where to find you."

"Maybe he changed his mind at the end." I had a faint memory of calling out for my BB doll, which was so odd. While I always kept it with me, I didn't recall sleeping with her as a child. Did I call out for it as a memory or a distraction?

"Well, Miss Sammy, for whatever reason, we're glad he did. And now here's where I reprimand you for trespassing and..."

Detective Gammon entered the room. "Hold it, I'm the bad cop who does the trespassing speech."

I took a moment before answering her as her attire surprised me. Instead of the usual suit, she was dressed in dark blue jeans and a black T-shirt. She still looked polished, so I assumed this was her version of business casual. "I deserve it. Are you here to arrest me?"

"I should," she said. She started off with a serious look, but she didn't keep it for long. A smile that I hadn't seen before brightened her face. "But under the circumstances I asked the church not to press charges. I explained it was a complicated situation, and you meant no harm. And you are a tomb owner. They ask that you only come to your family mausoleum during open hours."

Surprised at the news, I stuttered out, "Th-thank you. And I promise not to do it again."

"You're welcome. And yes, don't do it again," she said. "My vault is just two rows from yours. I'll see you around, Sammy." And with that she left the room.

"Well, now you've got to stay. Christine didn't arrest you and she called you Sammy. You're one of us now." Rob grinned as the door closed behind his partner.

"I wasn't planning on leaving, especially if Christine isn't running me out of town."

Rob stood up and came over to the bed. "Good! Before I go, as a detective, I'll offer that when we have more information about Joey, we'll share it with you. And that you need to stay out of trouble."

"Thank you. I'll be on the straight and narrow from now on."

"As your friend, if you want to learn about your past, we're all here to support you. And don't look for trouble. No more dolls, diaries, or keys, okay?" He kissed me on the cheek and left the room.

I lay back in my hospital bed, exhausted and relieved. I wanted no more dolls, diaries, or keys. Or drama. Or attempted murder. Or real murders. All I wanted was to put the past behind me...at least for now.

62

"Sammy, here's your key. We're so happy you're home," Libby said as she opened my door. She and William had insisted on bringing me back from my hospital stay.

"Thanks, Libby. I appreciate y'all driving me," I said as I accepted my apartment key from her once again.

"She's already saying y'all. Sammy, you'll be a true Southerner sooner rather than later," William teased as he set my bag in my bedroom.

"See, I knew from day one she would fit right in," Libby said as she put groceries away. "Frankie insisted on sending food over. She and Frank send their best. Especially Frank."

"Your mail is on the counter, and once Libby's finished we'll be out of your hair."

"I'm done. You rest now, darling," Libby cooed as she and her husband walked out the door. "Oh, Miss Ruby, hello. Who is that with you?"

I joined them to find my neighbor there with a large bag and a wriggling black cat with a distinctive white circle of fur on her head.

"This is Samantha's; at least that's what Andrew told me," Ruby said as the kitty jumped out of her arms. "He's from the cemetery, and Sissy said you claimed him."

I picked up my furry friend. "She helped me at the graveyard, and I guess in my concussion-induced haze, I declared her mine. Is it okay, Libby?"

"Of course it is! What a sweet little thing." She and William left, leaving Ruby and me alone.

"Thank you for taking care of her, Miss Ruby."

"I had no choice. Andrew is apparently allergic to cats," she said. "But I will say he is a lovely cat, and Cleopatra and Nefertiti enjoy his company."

"I'm glad to hear that. I guess she needs a name."

"I named him. He's Anubis. Your cat is a he."

"Oh. Why Anubis?"

"Anubis is the god of the afterlife. I thought it appropriate considering your story."

I couldn't argue with that. "Okay, then. Welcome to my apartment, Nubi." I let my new friend in, and he settled on my love seat to nap.

"It's Anubis." She sighed. "Have some respect for proper names."

"I will, I promise," I said with a straight face, which wasn't easy as I looked at the annoyed woman in front of me. Perhaps this was the beginning of an understanding between us. Not a friendship, necessarily, but maybe we would at least tolerate each other.

"Good. Now here are his things and a list of instructions. Please follow them. I don't want any trouble for Anubis."

"I agree. I don't want any trouble for me either."

Ruby studied my face and then spoke. "Your cat won't be any concern for you, but I sense there is more unrest heading your way."

"Do you see Joey returning?" I couldn't believe I was asking a tarot card reader about him, but there was no sign of him since the cemetery.

"Your brother? I can't see what is in store for you, but be careful. If not for you, for those who live by you."

Now, there was the Ruby I knew. "Thanks for taking care of Anubis. I'll try to stay out of trouble."

She gave a curt nod and brushed the fur from her yellow chiffon robes as if she needed a moment. She began walking away but not before I heard her mumble under her breath, "Losing family is hard, my dear, even if they're no good."

I didn't have to ask her what she meant.

After closing my door, I grabbed the mail off the counter and sat next to Nubi on the love seat. He was already at home having stretched his lean body across half the couch.

"Thanks for sharing." I laughed as I scratched the top of his head.

Among the bills and magazines was an unmarked envelope. I ripped it open to find just a dog-eared photo. It shook in my hands as I stared at it.

Sitting on the steps of a French Quarter cottage, a strawberry-blonde toddler wore a pink smocked dress, and with one hand she gripped a BB doll. With her other hand, she reached into a box of Aunt Sally's pralines held by an older, brown-haired boy. He sported an ear-to-ear grin as he gazed down at the girl.

It was a charming photo, a glimpse of kids without a care in the world. I wish I could remember that day. I wish I could remember that happy child who adored his sister. I wish I could remember that smiling girl who loved her brother. I wish I knew that boy, not the man he became.

Was this photo a warning or an apology?

Eventually, I would find out which it was. And hopefully

I'd learn more about those two happy children and their family. I placed the photo along with the tomb key inside *The Clue of the Black Keys*, my favorite Nancy Drew book. My past would be there when I was ready.

I turned from the bookshelf after hearing a knock and finding Connor standing in my now open doorway.

"Hey. What are you up to?"

"Just putting stuff away," I said as I reached for his outstretched hand. "What are you up to?"

He pulled me outside. "Getting you for dinner."

Everyone from the apartment building, except Ruby, sat in the back of the courtyard. It reminded me of our first party there, and my heart sank as I thought of Matt. Kelly's death was tragic, but Matt's death would always haunt me. I hoped someday I could forgive my brother for the things he had done, but Matt's murder would never be one of them.

"It will be okay, Sammy; you're home now," Connor whispered.

"Come on, we've got a Pimm's cup waiting for you," Neal yelled from the bar by the fountain.

Connor gently pushed me forward, and I grabbed my drink from Neal and stood next to Sissy. I took a sip as I looked out on the group. Andrew raised his glass and declared, "A toast, my friends. To our past, our present, and our future. May we all find what we're looking for."

I smiled at Andrew, who always said the right things to me. My brother gave me more than just a key to my past; I had the key to my future. Standing with this group of former strangers, now I was part of a family. One day I would learn about my past, but for the present I was content with where I was, and that was the key to happiness in my book.

Sammy's adventures continue next in
the gates to the afterlife.

Sign up for Jen's newsletter for updates and more at
jenpittsauthor.com/newsletter

ACKNOWLEDGMENTS

Thank you to my husband, Dave, for always believing I was a writer even when I didn't. Your encouragement, creative, and technical skills keep me going as a writer, wife, mother, and human being. I love you and I promise not to kill any husbands in my novels.

To my children, Jack and Night, thank you for understanding when I'm absorbed with my writing. I hope that you see that you can reach for your dreams no matter how old or young you are. Your energy, your kindness, your intelligence, and your humor inspire me. I love you and you'll always be my babies.

Dad and Wanda, little did I know that among your many talents were proofreading and critiquing. Thank you for being two of my best cheerleaders. Get ready for more work because you're the first to read the new books. I love y'all.

Thanks to my BARN critique group for their advice with my novel as well as keeping me sane throughout the process. Amanda, Amelia and Doug, you continue to help me grow as a writer. Thank you for your feedback and friendship.

Katy and Jenna, thank you for agreeing to be my beta-readers. Your insights were invaluable and I hope I can call on you again. Thank you for being part of my journey as well as being good friends.

Thank you to my cousins, Alex and Donna Marie, for

showing me your favorite parts of New Orleans. I loved spending time with you. I love y'all.

My love of mysteries began with my Nancy Drew books and Agatha Christie novels. My love of New Orleans started with the book *Interview with the Vampire* and then my first trip to New Orleans. Thank you for all those things and more, Mom and Priscilla. I love you both.

Thank you to my friends and family, near and far. Whether it was in person, through emails or on Facebook, the encouragement everyone gives means the world.

It takes a village to raise a child, but also to raise a writer.

ABOUT THE AUTHOR

Jen Pitts is a lifelong mystery reader who turned her obsession into writing cozy mysteries of her own. When she isn't plotting fictional murder, she's chugging coffee, traveling to New Orleans, reading, and enjoying life with her husband, children, and two cats in the Pacific Northwest.

Learn more about Jen through her newsletter. A free short story prequel is available exclusively for newsletter members. Sign up at www.jenpittsauthor.com

And keep up daily with Jen on Facebook where she shares her books, her cats, and her love of New Orleans.

You can also find Jen on the following social media sites:

facebook.com/jenpittsmysteryauthor

instagram.com/jenpittsmysterywriter

goodreads.com/jenpitts

amazon.com/author/jenpitts

bookbub.com/authors/jen-pitts

ALSO BY JEN PITTS

The French Quarter Mystery Series:

Coffee, a Scone, and a Place to Call Home - a Short Story Prequel

The Key to Murder

The Gates to the Afterlife

A Deadly Check-In

Bury the Past

The Dead End Tour

A Corpse in the Cafe

Happy Homicide

A Courtyard Conundrum

The Witches of the French Quarter Series:

Mardi Gras and Magic

Red Beans and Rituals

Alligators and Apparitions

Chicory and Charms